A Bane in Salem

A Tale of the Salem Witch Trials

By L. M. Roth

Table of Contents

Chapter 1
A Crusader's Quest

It was the spots that gave her away. In years to come they would always remember that; it was the spots. And the fact that she went to old Biddy Merriweather, the wise woman, to get a cure to get rid of those spots. And then, of course, there was that silly game the girls played, looking into water to see the faces of their future husband. Had it not been for that, Salem may never have exploded the way that it did.

But always, Letitia would remember, the deadly bane would always be to blame; all the trails led back to the poison that caused Salem's downfall.

As she pondered along the road on this foggy October night as the sun was just beginning to set and the mists of autumn settled among the trees, those trees that were now beginning to shed their leaves, their autumn canopy of glory leaving only the bare stark outlines of trees until the first snowfall came, she remembered. And she rued.

She rued the day she had listened to Temperance and sought out Biddy Merriweather. And she rued obeying her mother's orders instead of following her heart. And then there was the one who betrayed her, the one who waited in secret for the moment to strike, and when it came did so with a vengeance, as surely as an asp lying in wait for its intended victim.

But in this matter her assailant was no different from those others who had lashed out their slander against the innocent from the venom that infected them. And the venom went deep, deep into the souls of those who accused them, those who gloated seeing the life taken from them. Those who would later remember the massacre at Salem, those who had initiated it, those who had called for it, those who had gloried in it once it had taken place.

But others in the years to come would question; what really happened at Salem? Why the outbreak of hysteria? And were those who were hanged really to blame? Were they innocent; or had they been falsely accused by those who simply had looked for an excuse to bring about their extermination?

Such were the questions of those who years later would conduct an investigation and wonder; why had this happened? How had it come about?

Salem was a divided community, one that was well-known for its factions and quarrels; a characteristic that was ironic in view of the fact that its name meant peace, and was shortened from Jerusalem with the intention of establishing a city of God in the New World. It was split into two separate divisions: Salem Village and Salem Town. Salem Town was composed primarily of merchants and lay on the rugged coast of the North Shore and at the mouth of the Naumkeag River. It was established on the site of an ancient Indian Village in the year 1629 and quickly became a vital port in the budding New England Colonies.

Salem Village was located on the Danvers River not far from the North Coast, but was primarily a farming community of about five hundred people, many of whom felt inferior to the more cultured citizens of Salem Town, an opinion which was largely shared by the inhabitants of Salem Town. In Salem Village itself the townsfolk were inclined to quarrel, and it did not take much for arguments to break out. Nothing was deemed too petty to fight over, whether it was property lines, grazing rights for livestock, feuds among families, or privileges among church members. So divided was the community that Salem Village had gone so far as to hire their own minister, not wishing to share one with Salem Town.

Such was the unpleasant bickering of the village, however, that the first two ministers only lasted a few years. The first minister, James Bayley, left after four years of grievous attempts to reconcile the citizens to Salem Town and to one another. As the citizens declined to pay him his full wages, he felt fully justified in leaving them to settle their differences on their own, or to live with the consequences of their discord.

The Reverend George Burroughs encountered similar strife, and also failed to secure his full payment in wages. Like his predecessor, he felt released to take his leave of the quarrelsome community and leave them to whatever fate the hand of God saw fit to send them. But the Reverend Burroughs would never be free of Salem Village, and a dark fate awaited him at a future time.

A third man of God had a different issue with Salem Village. The church in Salem refused to ordain him, although he served them for a little over three years and did his best to show the love of God to the community. In what amounted to a rejection by those he had labored to love, the Reverend Deodat Lawson took his leave and shook the dust of Salem Village off of his shoes as he did so. But he could never bring himself to abandon the people of it entirely and was willing to rush to their aid in time of need; so deeply rooted was the love of God for them in that good man's heart.

It would be left to the fourth minister hired by Salem Village to take on the burden of ministering to this difficult parish. Reverend Samuel Parris was hired for an agreed wage, provisions, and the use of a parsonage to house himself and his family, which included his young daughter Betty and his orphaned niece Abigail Williams, who between the two of them would one day make Salem famous.

There were darker rumors of Salem as well. Those who knew it well whispered of haunted woods surrounding Salem Village, and of those who met there on certain nights to practice mysterious rituals and execute dark deeds. Witchcraft, it was said, had a secret following in this Puritan enclave, and there were those who worshiped the devil in secret and did his bidding. That bidding, so it was said, was to undermine and sabotage the true believers who had come to establish God's kingdom on earth in the American Colonies.

Some scoffed at the rumors and declared it superstition muttered by those who were afraid of their own shadow and saw evil in everything. But there were others who stated that the woods were mysterious after nightfall, and that they hastened through them when forced to travel through them after the sun had set. And what of the virulent quarreling and bickering of the Salem community; was that not evidence enough of the devil's minions spreading strife and discord to break the harmony of a Christian fellowship?

Only time and evidence, it was said, would prove whether the rumors of witchcraft be true or false.

All over New England, he cried out for their blood. Whether they were young and comely or old and haggard, it did not matter to Cotton Mather. He was on a campaign. He was determined to stamp out witchcraft throughout the New England Colonies, where he was certain that it had gained a foothold and threatened the citizens who desired to live godly lives in a manner that pleased their Maker.

The Puritans of the Massachusetts Colony were firm believers in the supernatural, demonic possession, and the existence of witches who delighted in casting spells that harmed their fellow townsfolk. It was a belief that they brought with them from their native England and one that was largely shared throughout Europe, when the Burning Times had decimated entire villages in the zeal to exterminate evil. In Massachusetts was founded a community that constantly exercised a vigil over the influence of malevolent powers, and was exactly the fertile ground that the seeds of the Crusade would be planted in to one day reap a bitter harvest.

From his citadel in the city of Boston the Reverend Cotton Mather published pamphlets that warned the citizens throughout the Colonies of the dangers of witchcraft, most notably in his book Memorable Providences Relating to Witchcrafts and Possessions. He shared his personal observations of its power, and described in great and harrowing detail how the forces of evil had affected the children of a Boston man named John Goodwin, inciting these innocents to do wicked deeds.

One of the children had allegedly been tempted to steal linens from Goody Glover, a washerwoman by trade, who was accused of casting spells on the Goodwin children. Not only were they incited to do wrong, but they endured physical attacks on their bodies, which caused them to flap their arms, suffer pains in their necks and backs, lose control of their tongues, and make them cry out in agony.

Such was clearly the result of witchcraft afflicted on the vulnerable who could not defend themselves, Mather proclaimed, and it must be exterminated from the environs of the Colonies. Oh, yes, the agency of the devil must be exposed and driven out, he thundered from the pulpit on a righteous Crusade, this man of God who was so stern of appearance, so rigid in his manner, so unrelenting in his quest to uproot evil and dismantle it. The citizens of Boston gave him their full attention and read his pamphlets voraciously, and examined their own households for any sign that witchcraft had gained a foothold.

And it was no exception in the Village and Town of Salem, Massachusetts, where they heard of his thunderous sermons, applauded his righteous zeal, and were willing to aid and abet him in his pursuit throughout the New England Colonies. But there was no Colony more zealous than that of Massachusetts, the very cradle of liberty, where the Puritans had followed the Pilgrims on their quest for religious freedom and had come so many years earlier and founded a New World.

Let it begin here; let the pursuit of righteousness and the eradication of evil begin here where it all began. Let it be said in the generations to come that the righteous citizens of Massachusetts would not brook any pact with the devil. Let it be said that the good and pious citizens of Massachusetts served a righteous and holy God, and showed no mercy to those who perpetuated the enemy's agenda.

And so it was that Cotton Mather, that zealot, that blazing eyed fanatic, found the very people that could perpetuate his campaign.

Chapter 2
The Girl Who Was Different

None of this was on the mind of Letitia, however, as she tripped along merrily through the September fields. Oh, how she loved to just take a walk in the woods and through the meadows, listening to birds' songs, capturing butterflies, sniffing the wildflowers, and in general just enjoying the beauty of God's creation. All around her in the beauty He created she saw evidences of His glory that caused her to lift up her heart in spontaneous worship to the One who had given her life.

She sometimes wondered as she listened to the sermons in the Meeting House every Sunday why the minister preached a different God than the One she read of in God's Holy Word. He seemed so loving, so caring, so giving, and forgiving. Yes, He was holy and without sin; but the God she read about seemed to love His children and had infinite patience with them. And for her there was nowhere closer that she could feel Him than in the beauty of His creation.

And so she would skip along through the fields, raising her skirts and jumping for joy, singing in exultation, behaving like anything but the young lady that she was expected to be. But then Letitia had always been different from the other maidens of Salem Village. Many of them puzzled over her odd behavior and bizarre remarks she made in regards to faith and life that differed so greatly from what their elders had taught them and they obediently believed. Her mother had dared to give her a name that was different from the names of so many of the other girls of her acquaintance. They had names like Mercy, Remembrance, Chastity, Temperance, Humility, and Prudence, along with the Biblical names of Mary, Sarah, Deborah, Abigail, and Ruth.

And her mother had dared to call her Letitia. That alone set her apart and caused people to whisper about her as she passed through the lanes of the small village of Salem. That fact alone made the young men look at her askance, as though she were different from the other maidens.

But in what way was she different? Was she unchaste? Was she better than they? They did not know, but agreed among them when they discussed Letitia that something about her set her apart.

Letitia's mother once told her of the scandalous reactions she evoked from the ladies of the village when she had chosen her name.

"Letitia; I chose Letitia for you, and you would have thought the world had ended," she clucked as she explained to her then thirteen year old daughter the origin of her unusual name.

"What was so shocking about it?" Letitia asked her mother.

Secretly she thought it was a pretty name and was glad that her mother had chosen one that was unusual and different from those of the other girls. She would have hated to have an ordinary name, especially one that was so common in the village that she ran the risk of being confused with another maiden with the same name. Her mother, whose name was Ruth and named after the Biblical heroine, rolled her eyes and sighed deeply as she remembered back to the day she had scandalized the ladies of the village.

"What was so shocking is that the first person everyone thought of when they heard what I had christened you was Letitia Knollys," Ruth replied.

"Who was she?" her daughter asked.

Ruth flushed unexpectedly and looked slightly uncomfortable but proceeded with her story.

"Well, she wasn't the purest lady you would ever hold up as an example of virtue and modesty," Ruth said, clearing her throat before proceeding. "In fact, there are some who say she was a wicked woman.

"She was married three times and unfaithful to at least the first two, that much is known for certain, and is *not* mere rumor or idle gossip. She was first married to Walter Devereaux in an arranged marriage when she was very young, and then had an affair with Robert Dudley, the Queen's favorite, whom she elevated to the Earl of Leicester because of her love for him. After Letitia's husband Walter died she married Leicester and incurred the wrath of Queen Elizabeth, who called her a she-wolf, and hated her for the rest of her life, even though they were actually cousins and Letitia had previously been one of her ladies in waiting, and a close confidante. Letitia was the granddaughter of Mary Boleyn, a woman of loose morals who had been mistress to King Henry VIII (among others, it is said) before the King married her sister Anne; that is how she was related to the Queen.

"When Letitia felt that the Earl neglected her to dance attendance on the Queen, who actually banished her from the Court for her marriage to Dudley, she whiled away the time with Christopher Blount. In time the Earl died and she married Blount after the death of Dudley. We know nothing of any affairs that she had behind Blount's back, but it may be that by that time she was too old for such goings on.

"However, I did not think of her or any of her scandals when I named you: I just liked the name. But with these Puritans you would have thought the world had come to an end, or close to it."

And Ruth shook her head and clucked her tongue as she thought of her neighbors and their propensity to be scandalized by anything that was out of the ordinary.

Letitia knew that her mother had come from a different background than her Puritan husband, having been raised a Protestant in the tradition of the Church of England, although she hailed from Boston. She had met her husband John when he studied there at Harvard and attended a harvest celebration where she and her family were also present. They had fallen in love and for his sake she converted to his faith, although it was clear (to Letitia at least) that there were times when she seemed to rebel against it, or chafe at the narrow-mindedness of her Puritan neighbors.

Her younger sister had been named for Letitia Knollys' cousin, Queen Elizabeth, and had therefore escaped the censure that her own name had brought. However, as Elizabeth was a fairly common name throughout the Puritan community, she was always called by her middle name, Delilah. Although it was a name that raised eyebrows considering her Biblical namesake, Delilah was forgiven the origin of her name as the neighbors reminded each other that at least it came out of the Word of God, which was more than could be said for Letitia.

And so Letitia's sister did not endure the whispering that she did due to the origin of her name. For the Puritans saw symbolism in many things, and it was said that it was unfortunate for Letitia to share her name with a harlot. With such a namesake, what kind of future could be expected of her?

But Letitia rarely thought of the controversy her name stirred up among her neighbors. To her the name meant nothing in itself, and she shrugged her shoulders when thought of how it had shocked her neighbors when she was born. She was different in other ways, and in these she would not have changed herself for all the approval in the world.

For Letitia nothing could compare to the wonder and delight of walking through an autumn wood on a sunny afternoon, watching the light of the sun settling on the leaves and setting them ablaze so that they looked like jewels captured on the tree branches; or feeling the first snowfall on her cheeks, the softness of those downy white flakes transporting her back to the wonders of childhood. And wasn't the summer night better employed watching a full moon rise on the horizon, listening to the songs of the nightingales, mesmerized by the chirping of the crickets as they emerged from their August hiding places than going dutifully to bed at a proper hour and missing all of the enchantment of the twilight and the creatures that ushered its arrival with beautiful melodies?

Was this not better than being forced to listen to interminable sermons, all about what must be her sins, and yes, she *had* sins; she was not perfect. But did not God know this and forgive her of them? Had He not sent His Son Jesus to take on the sin of all mankind so that they could know the love of God and live with Him forever, as He had so fervently desired when He created Adam and Eve?

When Letitia read the account of Creation she saw, not a God who shook His finger at their wrongdoing, but One who grieved over what amounted to His children's rejection of Him when they ate the fruit to "be like God," as the lying serpent promised, knowing full well that such a thing was impossible even as he tempted them to challenge the One who made them. This was just as Lucifer had done when he revolted and led one third of the angels of Heaven with him in an effort to take God's throne, failing in the attempt and falling to earth below where they lost their glory and diminished to demons. Here on earth they preyed on mankind, hating those who had been created in the image of God, and seeking to destroy those in whom He delighted and loved. Adam and Eve had been the first victims to be led astray by the lies of the serpent, and the devil would be satisfied with nothing less than all out war on God's beloved children.

It was not so much the act as the motive behind the eating of the fruit that caused Man's fall, Letitia pondered when she read Genesis. They had been expelled for insubordination to His sovereignty in wanting to be God in their own eyes, and not for mere disobedience, she thought. In her opinion it was one thing if she were to sneak behind her father's back and do what she had expressly been forbidden to do, and another to reject him as her father, tantamount to denying that he had created her, and declaring that she was divine and accountable to no one but herself.

Was she wrong to see these things in the Word of God and to feel this way? Did she serve a different God than the One the preacher spoke of? She did not know; but as her conscience didn't smite her about it she thought she must be alright in her convictions.

However, as she passed through the village it was not uncommon for the old biddies to put their heads together and wag their tongues about the girl who was different. And just as she passed among them she saw other girls whispering, girls her age, girls that looked solemn of countenance and had their manes of golden hair and their crops of crisp black curls restrained in a white cap so that not even a stray strand would escape, the very embodiment of their elders, the very personification of prim little mistresses who would always do the right thing.

But as for Letitia, the road to righteousness came hard, and she wondered at times how she could bear it. She did all that was expected of her from her parents and the villagers, knowing that she would be severely criticized if she did not. There were times when she felt that she could not breathe, and would surely die of suffocation as her real self was repressed under a veneer of propriety; a repression that only increased as she approached marriageable age and must conform to the image of what was expected of a good and virtuous wife.

Every time a ship sailed into harbor she accompanied her father to buy goods from its cargo. She was there to watch its arrival, not because she knew anyone aboard, but because she wished to be one of the sailors on it. How exciting it would be to sail the world and see its beauties, to experience the diversity of lands and cultures so different from Salem, and to hear tales and songs from people who spoke languages that she had never heard before. In her spare time after her chores were done for the day she eagerly read books, finding in them adventure, romance, and the sense of a wider world with broader horizons and citizens with larger visions than the ones she knew.

As she watched the ships with many sails pull into the harbors she visualized being carried away on the breeze to far away islands and lands unknown. When she heard the splash of the waves against the side of a ship she heard the lapping of waves on tropical isles that knew no cold, where flowers grew year round, and the inhabitants ate the sweetest of fruits. The appearance of one sailor who was from the Orient but spoke perfect English brought to mind fragrant teas, exotic textiles that were never permitted to be worn in the severe Puritan village, and a sense of an ancient civilization far older than the one she lived in.

Such thoughts only deepened the frustration and longing within her, and her heart ached with the desire to be free to explore and experience all the wonders of the world that God had created. But the burning question that forever haunted her was; when could she flee the village and escape the imprisonment of her bondages?

Chapter 3
The Friendship

Life in the Colonies was not easy. It was not for the faint of heart or the lazy of body. Here the men had carved out an existence from the heavily forested land and fought with or made treaties with the native Indians who threatened their lives. While some of the native populace were friendly and greatly helped the colonists in settling into their new land, there were others who resented the invasion by the white man and campaigned against them, taking lives in retaliation for stolen land and ruined heritages.

One such raid had deprived young Abigail Williams, the niece of the local minster Reverend Samuel Parris, of her parents. A surprise attack had left her native village unprepared and her mother and father were slaughtered. She had no siblings and no other close family, so the Reverend and his wife took her in and adopted her as one of their own.

It was noted, discreetly due to the status of the little orphan's uncle, that the loss of her parents in such a violent way left the young girl with what appeared to be a nervous complaint. She was prone to jump whenever she heard an unexpected sound, and her eyes popped if something came into the range of her vision that she was unprepared for. She had a way of clutching her cloak about her as if for protection, but from what unseen threat that only she could see none could say.

Poor little thing, was the general opinion

expressed by the mistresses of the village, and they lavished attention and affection on her whenever they met her at meeting or around the town.

Delilah was a close friend of hers, as they were exactly the same age and Delilah's tender heart was roused with compassion for the plight of the other girl. Her mother looked on the friendship somewhat differently, saying that while it was to Delilah's credit to befriend a luckless orphan, there was something distinctly strange about Abigail that made her uneasy, and it was with reluctance that she allowed her daughter to befriend her.

"Oh, Mother, how can you say such a thing?" Delilah asked her one morning. "It is not Abigail's fault that her parents were murdered, and she forced to witness it. It was truly horrifying! You cannot imagine how terrifying it was. Had she not been unable to sleep and heard the attack begin and taken shelter in a cupboard, she too might have been butchered as they were. How could she *not* be scarred by such an ordeal?"

Letitia on hearing this exchange at the breakfast table one morning was inclined to agree with both her sister and her mother. It was sad and unfortunate for poor Abigail to lose her parents in such a way and to be left alone in the world except for the charity of her uncle. But she secretly agreed with her mother that there *was* something strange about the girl that set her apart from the other villagers, and inwardly made Letitia's skin crawl whenever she witnessed one of Abigail's nervous reactions to the unexpected.

At just that moment there was a knock at the back door. Ruth jumped up from the table to answer it. Those at the table heard her exchange words with someone, and then the sound of Ruth rummaging around in the kitchen came to their ears, and then the patter of Ruth's feet as she returned to the back door. A low murmuring voice was heard and then the door was quickly shut.

Ruth returned to the table with downcast eyes and sat down.

"Who was that?" her husband John asked.

Ruth looked slightly uncomfortable and hesitated before answering. She pulled at her ear lobe as if her cap bothered her and cleared her throat but did not respond to her husband's question. He glanced up at her.

"I repeat, wife; who was at the door?" he asked in a firm monotone that Letitia knew by experience demanded an answer.

Ruth licked her lips and put a hand to her chest over her heart.

"It was Sarah Good," she responded, and then asked Delilah if she had eaten her fill.

"Sarah Good?" John inquired.

His mouth became a hard straight line in his face and he scowled at his wife, who carefully avoided his eye.

"Yes, Sarah Good," Ruth repeated.

"And what business do we have with that filthy beggar?" he asked her, as his eyes never left Ruth's face.

"She needed something to feed her daughter," Ruth answered, clearly flustered by her husband's inquisition.

Her behavior was a surprise to Letitia, who secretly felt that her mother dominated her father. But in this instance she demonstrated that there were some things she hid from her husband, a surprising revelation to her daughter.

"And you gave it to her, I assume?" John asked.

He threw down his napkin and sighed in disgust.

"Woman, we have nothing to do with the likes of her; do you understand that?" he declared. "She is no good, nor is her husband. Good! What an ironic name; for it is rumored that she is a witch, and we do not truckle with any that be accused of such."

"She is not a witch," Ruth stated firmly, "just a woman who had the misfortune to marry a man who left her in debt, to such an extent that she and her second husband have lost their home in their attempts to settle it. They are even now living in the woods with a rough shelter, a mere tent as it were. Is that sufficient protection from the elements for anyone? And what of their little girl, Dorothy? Should we not show Christian compassion for such a poor family?"

"All in Salem shun them," her husband stated. "They beg from their neighbors, and when their request is not answered it is said by those who have witnessed it that Sarah curses them under her breath. And they know that she is muttering curses on those who deny her aid. We will not have any doings of any kind with that sort. Is that clear?"

He fastened his eyes unblinkingly on his wife, whose own faltered beneath his glare.

"It is clear," Ruth answered in a small voice.

She stared down at her plate and ate in silence. She was not accustomed to being shamed before her children, and both Letitia and Delilah suddenly rose from the table and began to clear off the dishes and prepare to wash them.

Letitia pondered on the incident later that afternoon when she walked by a favorite pond in a nearby meadow in her leisure time. It was a quiet place, where she loved to come and be alone, watching butterflies flit over the wildflowers in the summer, and listen to the calls of birds that did not frequent the woods, making the meadows their domain. On this day, in early autumn, cattails surrounded the short and the ducks had arrived to take a swim in the warmth that still lingered on the land. They clustered in groups and fighting erupted when one swam too close or threatened another's space. Their flapping wings sent showers of water into the air, the drops sparkling in the sunlight and sending a refreshing spray on Letitia's face.

She suddenly noticed a large swan that glided into view from the far side of the pond where it curved near a stretch of woods. The white bird sailed majestically among its smaller neighbors, and appeared to ignore their flapping wings and quacking scolds, as it carved a path of its own through the water merely by floating on its surface. Letitia was struck with an insight, that this was symbolic of peace, the ability to disregard agitation and conflict and remain fixed on a course of one's own, without being disturbed by any excitement that emanated from those who were riled with distress.

But even as she meditated on this revelation, she thought of the incident with Sarah Good and her mother's attempt to be kind to her, while her father shared in the general contempt of the village toward a woman whose only fault was to lose her home and all that she possessed in attempting to settle the debt that she regarded as her obligation. In this instance Letitia inwardly applauded her mother for daring to be like the swan that disregarded the quacking and quarrelsome ducks while it set out on a course of its own.

Yet she knew that her mother would have to cave in to the wishes of her father, and poor Sarah and her family would have ill luck trying to find charity in the community that judged her so harshly. And Letitia felt an unexpected kinship with this woman who, like herself, was not accepted as part of the norm.

But in all of Salem Village Letitia did have one good friend, a true ally, someone who would champion her no matter what the cost of doing so. She was a friend who exchanged confidences when they met at the stream to wash their family linen, who shared secret jokes when their eyes would meet during the long Sunday sermon and their lips curl and their eyes twinkle with amusement at the minister's expense, and who joined in her musings of the men that they would one day marry.

Her name was Constance Gable. She was true to her name; faithful, loyal, a stalwart friend, everything that a friend ought to be. And Letitia trusted her absolutely and unquestioningly. She knew with utter certainty that if ever she were in any difficulty that Constance would be there by her side, she knew that if she were ever in any danger that Constance would face it with her and find a way of escape. She expected that when the time came for her to marry that Constance would be her honorary attendant, the one who would escort her in her transition from maidenhood into the secrets, joys, and mysteries of matrimony. Of that she had no doubt.

They had always known each other. They had been born and raised in Salem Village and known each other all their lives, as had the other villagers who came before them, because few ever left their home village to settle elsewhere. Travel was difficult with such primitive roads, new territory to be taken was difficult due to the rugged and heavily forested terrain, and most preferred to live close to their extended families in time honored tradition. It was unthinkable that any of them would ever leave the confines of their village to move elsewhere.

For here was where the roots were; here was where their families were. And outside were dangers. Outside the villages were the Indians, always ready to rise up against them in retaliation for taking their lands. Outside the villages were the wolves that waited for hapless citizens to leave the safety of their towns and venture among them where they would make a nice tasty meal.

Letitia, like those who came before her, lived in the Village because her family did so, and unless she were to develop wings or receive some other miracle so that she could escape the confines of the Village, she would always live here. But she knew that as long as she had Constance at her side as a loyal friend that she would always be safe, because they would face difficulties together.

She thought about her now at this moment and wondered what she was doing. Was she too anticipating the harvest party that was set for next week? Was she, like Letitia, thinking of secrets to exchange around the bonfire where they warmed themselves on the cooling September evening? Was she also preparing to escape the confinement of girlhood and become a woman?

She wondered who their mates would be. She already knew that young Nathaniel Stone had his eye upon her, but she wasn't sure about him. Her eye was captured by another.

Chapter 4
Old Biddy Merriweather

Four days before the harvest party Letitia woke up to discover, greatly to her consternation, that her face was covered in red spots.

"Oh, dear," she murmured aloud. "How I loathe the very sight of these! No one will look at me as long as I have these spots all over my face, and there is no time to get rid of them before the party. Whatever shall I do?"

And while some of her more pious neighbors would no doubt say that it was an affliction from God that had to be borne (for was not everything that was inflicted on us, whether good or bad, directly from His hand and to be accepted without question?), she knew that no young man would look at her favorably as long as she had them.

And she had her eye on one young man in particular. So she racked her brain for some way to get rid of these spots. She tried to recall anything she had heard her mother or the other mistresses say about skin cures.

A potato buried in the ground to die? No, that was for wart removal, which would shrivel as the potato dried up. A tea applied to tone the skin? No, alas! that would only work for brightening the complexion, not for purifying it.

And then she remembered that one day when the maidens had assembled at the stream to wash laundry that she overheard Temperance Hale whisper to Chastity Morris that she had visited old Biddy Merriweather in secret to get a cure for the unsightly spots that marred her complexion.

"No! You did not dare!" Chastity whispered to her friend as her eyes widened and filled with delight at the audacity of such a deed.

Temperance giggled and glanced around to see whether anyone was listening. Letitia kept her eyes steadfastly on her laundry but her ears turned to their whispers. Seeing that all was apparently safe, Temperance continued.

"Aye, I did. But my spots cleared up in just a few days," she whispered. "I do not regret visiting her at all. Although I would not want my mother to know that I did such a thing," she added hastily.

But Letitia hesitated to do the same.

Biddy Merriweather was the old woman who lived just inside the edge of the wood that encircled Salem Village. She was dubbed a biddy because of her inability to get along with the other villagers, largely because of her refusal to conform to the behavior that was expected of her as a citizen of Salem. She was considered an outsider due to her removal from the confines of the village to the woods beyond, this by her own desire. She was not part of the village; she did not care to be part of the village, because she was too different.

She held no brook, she said, with any of these narrow-minded villagers and their rigid prejudices. She could not hold with their beliefs, she declared, and would not pretend to do so in order to court their favor and acceptance. All she wanted, she claimed, was to live her life in her way, and be free to pursue whatever she wanted to pursue, and the devil take the reckoning.

But it was grudgingly admitted even by some of the mistresses of the village, (always the harshest critics of any unusual behavior that they deemed to be out of order) that she seemed to know what she was doing in regards to herbs. And although none would dare admit it, there was many a Salem matron that would visit her secretly when their babies had fevers that wouldn't break, when their husbands had persistent coughs that wouldn't leave their chests, and they felt the rheumy ache in their own bones that made their unending housework difficult to perform. Many of them slipped on the sly to visit Biddy Merriweather for one of her unfailing cures.

Old Biddy Merriweather with her magic herbs (and some said her secret incantations and formulas that none would dare acknowledge but was always whispered and rumored of) was a mystery to Salem, and therefore considered an outsider. Some even said she was a witch, and it was for this reason that she did not attend meeting as the rest of them did with unfailing duty every Sunday. Which was the reason she had left the village to begin with; frustrated with their narrow-mindedness and tired of the rumors, she fled them to live her own life.

But Letitia thought of her now and wondered if she could help. So she made her way secretly under the cover of night, creeping out after her father, mother, and younger sister had all fallen soundly asleep. She made her way in stealth to the home of Biddy Merriweather.

She waited until nightfall. She did not dare to be seen going to the house of old Biddy Merriweather, as to do so would be to invite gossip and speculation for the reason for the visit.

She would be ostracized if she were found out, considered strange, considered rebellious, considered even more different than she already was. Letitia waited until the cessation of any movements from the bedchamber of her parents ensured that they had fallen asleep, until her sister Delilah was slumbering peacefully in the bed next to her own, her even breathing indicating pleasant dreams as she snuggled her cheek against her hand; and then she crept out by the back door and across the field under cover of the darkness. Fortunately, there was no moon that evening to betray her movements or reveal her silhouette in the pale light of its beams, and she fled into the shadows of the trees into the forest that bordered Salem Village.

It was an ancient forest that had lain undisturbed until the coming of the white man, who had dug out part of it to build a village. It still boasted trees of great height with dense foliage; towering pines with their fragrant needles and decorative cones that brightened the winter landscape, maples that flamed bright red in the autumn, elms that provided welcome shade in the heat of summer, and dogwoods that blossomed with fragile flowers in the spring. Moss clustered on the trunks of some of the older trees that bordered a wide stream that wound its way throughout the forest. Lichens adorned the ground in spots, turning it into ribbons of emerald green carpet from which tiny blue forget-me-nots spilled splashes of bright color to relieve the unrelenting green. All of this was a familiar sight to Letitia by daylight, for the forest was a favorite refuge of hers, where she often came to enjoy the solitude and revel in the beauty of its unspoiled wildness.

Now, however, all was dark, with no moon to light her way. But once she was in the woods she breathed much easier, feeling secure in its shelter from any curious eyes that might happen to witness her movements. She straightened her posture and walked erectly, taking deep breaths as she did so. It took a few minutes for her eyes to adjust to the blackness of the trees and the deep shadows that engulfed them. She lingered for a moment, inhaling the scent of the pine trees and lifting her face to the caressing night breeze that wafted gently through the boughs, and then trod softly and picked her way carefully along a path that wound through the wood.

After she became accustomed to her surroundings she looked around and admired the beautiful September night with the softness of the gentle breeze and the sound of the crickets chirping merrily in the woods. Here and there came the sound of a loon wailing mournfully from a pond not far distant, in which it was joined by a frog that seemed to commiserate with a plaintive cry of its own. Other frogs added their voices and soon there was a chorus of beautiful music ringing through the early autumn night and ascending to the heavens. Letitia stopped in her tracks and listened for a moment.

How lovely, she thought, how beautiful. Only in nature could harmonies be so perfect. It was a pity, she thought, that more did not appreciate the beauty of the natural world around them, especially those who claimed to be always thinking of the world to come.

She thought of her mother who thought only of the clothes on her back to be cleaned and cared for, and her home to be kept in order, and food to be prepared that she might fulfill her duty in feeding her family. Truthfully, though, Puritan clothes were utilitarian and did not require a great deal of upkeep as did the finery of other cultures with their more luxurious wardrobes. They did not garb themselves in bright colors and did not trim their garments with laces or ribbons as was fashionable in other societies. Most Puritan ladies wore shades such as navy blue, deep purple, brown, or dark green. Red or pink would have been considered shocking, and it would have been thought scandalous to wear such bright hues.

She thought that even her deep forest green meeting dress was pushing the boundaries a little bit, especially as she trimmed it with a cream colored collar and cuffs that softened her complexion and made it glow, and not with the traditional stark white that was intended to symbolize purity donned by the other maidens and mistresses. Letitia wore a matching cap on which she had discreetly embroidered in dark green thread leaves that bordered the frame around her face. She knew that when she went into meeting that people looked at her and whispered for daring to wear such an audacious cap.

But she could not help it; she had brilliant green eyes that went well with her copper colored hair and she enjoyed bringing out the color of them. She thought it was pathetic that any attempt to beautify oneself was considered sinful. And yet, that was the way the villagers looked on it.

Best to be plain than to be considered a painted harlot, was the general consensus among the mistresses.

Whether the men thought so or not was an issue to be debated; for surely, Letitia thought, they wanted to look at something pretty, something that gave them pleasure and brightened their eyes, and not at a woman who bore a resemblance to a weather-beaten old barn robbed of its vibrancy through its wearing down by the elements that assailed it.

After all, hadn't the patriarchs in the Bible married beautiful woman? And had not Esther had to undergo a beauty treatment before she was deemed fit to be presented to King Xerxes, even to the adornment added by the wearing of cosmetics? Why then, did the Puritans insist on plain attire and suppress any attempt on the part of their womenfolk to look attractive?

But here once more Letitia was confronted with the difference between what she was taught and what the Word of God actually said. And for that perplexity she had no answer to her questions.

Chapter 5
Spots and Spells

Before she knew it she came to old Biddy Merriweather's hut. It was a little house nestled in the woods, hardly more than a shack made out of old timbers. Letitia found herself wondering how the old woman even kept warm in the winter; it looked so flimsy, as if the first puff of wind from a gale would blow it away. And yet the woman lived here snug and content, defying the wind, the villagers, the elements themselves, and lived her own life in her own way and found happiness.

Letitia knocked carefully on the door and waited for the old woman to come, even now tempted to change her mind and flee back to the village before it was discovered that she was missing. She wondered whether she had time to turn back before the old woman heard her knock. Perhaps she was deaf and had not heard it. She felt her courage desert her, but just as Letitia was about to leave the door opened slowly.

Biddy Merriweather did not have very many visitors. She was used to most of them coming at night, and so she did not retire until well after midnight because she never knew when someone might come to her in secret seeking her aid, and she truly did desire to serve those who dared to do so, and be available for their needs. It was the only contact she had with the villagers except for when she ventured into the town to buy what the woods could not provide for her, and independent though she was, she relished the contact with other people, the only alleviation of her loneliness.

And so when she heard Letitia's timid knock it was not long before she came to the door and opened it wide to admit her into her humble hut.

There was a warm fire going, because on this early September night once the sun set a chill came in the air that brought with it a hint of the autumn to come. Letitia was somewhat cold after her walk and the sight of the fire crackling on the hearth made her forget her timidity and she scurried inside. She looked around her and saw the cheerful fire and bright rag rugs on the wooden floor. She felt tongue-tied, not knowing what to say to this mysterious woman, to whom she had never spoken, although she had seen her in the village on the rare occasions when Biddy ventured into it.

Biddy seemed to understand the girl's hesitancy, however, and shed a warm smile upon her.

"Sit down, lass, sit down," she said. "Here, take a seat on the stool by the fire and warm yourself."

Letitia willingly did as she bade and immediately put her hands out to the fire and warmed them. She sighed as her fingertips thawed and warmth spread down to her toes, and she waited for Biddy to continue. But Biddy waited for the maiden to speak and a twinkle sparkled in her ancient eyes, surrounded by deep wrinkles that seemed to frame them like windows in an abandoned old house.

Neither of them spoke for several minutes, each one waiting for the other to break the silence. Letitia heard an owl hooting in a tree nearby, and thought that Biddy resembled that creature a great deal with her hooded eyes, gray hair that stood up at the back of her head, and several whiskers that were clearly visible on her chin. She stared at the old woman and then realized it was rude of her and hastily dropped her eyes.

At last Biddy spoke and broke the silence.

"What brings you here, lass? Why have you paid me such a visit?"

Letitia looked at her, surprised that the old woman could not see the obvious. Did she not see the spots on her face? Why else would a young girl visit a woman with a reputation for healing?

"It's these spots," she said, pointing to her face. "I want to be rid of them and I heard that you have herbs and lotions that will remove them."

"Spots, you say?" old Biddy Merriweather cackled. "Ah, and why do you young girls be wanting to remove your spots? What is the harm in them, I say? It's just nature's way of releasing poison out of your system. That's all it is."

"But they are horrible!" Letitia exclaimed, finally recapturing her spirit as she was reassured by the gruffness of the old woman. "They mar the complexion, no one will look at me, and..."

"No one will look at you?" questioned Biddy Merriweather. "Is that really so, lass?

Why, I hear that you are rather popular with the young men of the village."

She cackled again and slapped her hand upon her knee as if enjoying a good joke, but upon whom, Letitia could not say. She gasped at old Biddy's statement. Where had she heard such a thing?

Then she paused to think. It was true that she had attracted the attention of Nathaniel, who just two weeks ago had started waiting for her after the meeting, bowed in front of her, removed his hat, and said, "Good day, Miss Wood, and how do you fare?"

Letitia did not expect this, as Nathaniel was the most sought after young man in the village. He was seven years older than she, but had not yet married, or even courted anyone. All of the maidens looked at him with hopeful expectations. His father was an upstanding citizen with a fine lineage and a prosperous income from his trade, which was that of a blacksmith, one that Nathaniel helped him in with the intention of one day taking it over.

Letitia had to admit that Nathaniel was indeed handsome to look upon, possessing large brown eyes that radiated warmth, thick dark hair that many a maiden would have loved to stroke for the feel of its silky smoothness, and a pleasing countenance that brought a smile to the face of all who beheld it. But why he would look at Letitia with favor she had no idea.

Her friend Constance had stiffened beside her when he addressed her, no doubt as puzzled as Letitia was by this sudden attention from the most eligible bachelor in Salem Village.

But it had not stopped there. The next Sunday he had waited to escort her into the meeting on the steps of Meeting House. It was not a large building, but adequate to hold those who attended; it was one story high and was constructed entirely of wood. It lacked the decorative touches that were common to English churches, as the Puritans insisted on modesty.

Although the men had to sit separately from the women, with the men on one side of the room and the women on the other, Nathaniel still escorted her to a seat on one of the long wooden pews. He spoke a few pleasant words to her and then went on his way to join the men. He then waited to speak to her afterward and wish her a good day. The exchanges were not long, but the attention was making her nervous, especially as she had someone else in mind; someone whom no one knew she was interested in, and she was certain that she had attracted his eye as well...

But Biddy was speaking now.

"Remove those spots, you say? Why do you want to do that? Better to have the poison work itself out of your system than to keep it inside. Then you would be like too many of the villagers!" she cackled.

Letitia found herself laughing in agreement before she could restrain herself, knowing exactly what Biddy meant. It was true that there were some citizens in the village who were pious to one's face but very poisonous behind one's back. And she did not know which irritated her the most; the false piety or the poisonous remarks that made nothing of destroying a woman's reputation, or casting doubt on a man's courage, or deriding the appearance of one's home.

Truly, she thought, the old woman has hit on a kernel of truth with that statement.

"Well," said Biddy, "I expect you will be wanting me to remove these then."

"Yes," Letitia said, relieved that the old woman finally stopped teasing her. "I understand that you have herbs that will remove them."

"Herbs?" inquired Biddy. "Or do you want a spell?"

"A spell?" Letitia exclaimed, horrified at the suggestion. "Why would I want a spell? You are not a..."

"A witch?" asked Biddy.

She laughed again heartily, chuckling so hard that she began to wheeze and cough until she slapped herself on the back to stop it.

"No, no, no," she gasped through tears streaming down her face, "I am not a witch, but in the village you would think I am. It has been said that I cast spells on cattle, and bewitch the townsfolk, and send curses on the children.

"No, no; I am not a witch. I would not cast a spell on you, lass. But a potion I would give you with herbs, good healthy herbs, God's medicine indeed," she said. "Now allow me to fetch one for you; I have just the very thing in my cupboard."

She left the fireplace and went into the kitchen that opened off of the main room. Letitia heard her fumbling around in a cupboard. She quickly returned with a small glass bottle not much larger than Letitia's index finger that was stoppered with a tiny cork.

"Here you go, lass. Just put some of this on your face before you go to bed at night and within three days the spots will dry up and disappear. Then your complexion will be smooth again."

"Thank you so much!" Letitia cried. "What do I owe you in payment?"

"Ah, nothing!" said old Biddy. "Glad for the company, I am. Just keep yourself safe and Godspeed to you, lass."

Letitia smiled her thanks once again, and dropped a curtsy to the old woman and hastened from her hut.

As she walked along through the woods she tripped along merrily humming a little tune under her breath before she hastily caught herself. It was not wise to draw attention to one's presence in the woods after nightfall. It was only too easy to attract a predator that might be circling an intended victim in a hunt for prey.

She remembered the incident only a few years ago when a young boy only three years old had wandered off shortly before sunset on an October day. The parents had not noticed his absence at first in the midst of doing the evening chores, having seven children in all it was difficult at times to keep track of them all. It was only as they prepared to put the rest of the children to bed for the night that they discovered he was missing. They searched frantically and raised a hue and cry among their neighbors.

A group of men was sent to scour the

forest when the lad failed to turn up in the village. He was not found until the next day, the victim of a hungry bear, judging by the claw that had been left in his leg when he no doubt attempted to escape the grasp of the beast. Letitia shuddered as she remembered the horror of that discovery, and how the neighbors had come together in a rare moment of bonding to comfort the shocked and grieving family.

And then she heard something behind her.

What was that, she thought, as her heart began to pound rapidly, so quickly that she felt she would faint as dizziness assailed her.

She listened and then she heard the sound again; the sound of a twig breaking under someone's foot, coming from behind her. She whirled around but saw no one. Yet it was too big to be that of a squirrel or a fox stepping on a twig in the night. She thought of the deer scampering through the forest in the night, and of wolves roaming around seeking something to devour.

She began to perspire heavily and felt cold all over. She started trembling and her teeth chattered suddenly in her mouth, so violently that she had to put a hand to her jaw and clamp it tightly shut to stop them. Her breath felt strangled in her throat, and she gasped, stifling the sound lest she be heard.

But it was not a wolf. She saw nothing.

She held her breath and walked very stiffly, very quietly, clutching her skirts firmly to her side lest they rustle and betray her presence, trying to make as little noise as possible as she made her way back to her home. Indeed, she could not breathe again until she had let herself quietly in the back door and crept softly into her room and laid herself down on her bedding of linens stuffed with straw.

Strange, she thought before she drifted off into a fitful and uneasy sleep. I could swear that someone was following me.

Chapter 6
Revelry and Romance

It was the middle of September. The days with their intense blue skies piled with layers of fluffy white clouds that seemed stacked to the heavens were growing a little shorter, and noticeably cooler; but the breezes that came softly on the wind were refreshing. Letitia enjoyed them, so refreshing after the stifling heat of the summer.

She did not like hot weather very much. She enjoyed the golden sunshine that dispersed the gloomy skies after a thunderstorm, and the beauty of the flowers that grew in the field, and the soft grass that she secretly liked to run through after removing her shoes once she was well out of sight of the villagers. But she did not like the humidity and the heat that made her gown stick to her body and made it feel heavy and impeded her progress as she scampered through the meadows and the woods.

But September was welcome. Letitia didn't even mind the thought of what came after with winter following on the heels of autumn. She enjoyed the pristine snow that blanketed the fields and covered the forest floor with a white carpet that hushed the sounds of the woodland, the big fluffy flakes that fell softly from gray skies, the long cold nights that induced deep and refreshing slumber as she burrowed under her pile of pelts, the blazing fire on the hearth and the opportunities to read by the fireplace, and the cessation of her hard work outdoors during the summer months giving her leisure to read to her heart's content.

No, she did not mind September at all.

She left her house and hurried along to meet Constance, who emerged from her home wearing a dark blue gown with only her white collar and cuffs to relieve it, her little white cap sitting sedately on her head and almost completely covering her fine blond hair, and succeeded in subduing the unruly wisps that tended to curl around her face and lie on the nape of her neck.

"Are you ready?" Letitia asked her friend, barely able to contain her excitement.

"Yes, I am ready," Constance responded in the same spirit, her blue eyes sparkling with anticipation.

They linked arms companionably and walked arm in arm merrily down the path to the village square, where the young people were going to have a harvest party. They were bringing in the corn from the fields, vegetables from their gardens, berries from the woods, and apples from the orchards. This was the time of year when the young people made merry and celebrated. Their elders allowed them to have their own party, which was well chaperoned by at least a dozen of the more upstanding ladies of the community.

The village enjoyed their social gatherings, and held them regularly with the turning of the seasons and the festivals of the Church calendar. Some of this was frowned on by the more conservative inhabitants of Salem, who preferred that Christmas celebrations be outlawed, as they had been under Oliver Cromwell in England and in the New England Colonies until revoked by Governor Andros just ten years ago.

The villagers also frowned on drama, believing that such play-acting was an instrument of the devil, and the playing of cards which was an idle occupation at best, and when played for money was an opportunity for evil of all kinds. Indeed, those who indulged in gambling were derided as imprudent and rash; for why should anyone take chances with their hard-earned money that was better spent on the necessities of life? Should not one be content with what they had and be grateful for it, rather than take a gamble on increasing it, only to risk losing it?

But it was with gusto that Salem indulged in their celebrations.

The ladies prepared game and wild boar for the main course, and added freshly baked bread, corn, and the cranberries that grew so abundantly, along with other seasonal fruits and vegetables. Mead was a popular drink, along with beer and wine, it being firmly believed that alcohol was a good preventative for illness when taken in moderation; and the honey in the mead was widely believed to be a panacea for many woes.

But tonight belonged to the youth; it was their night. They were permitted to play music and dance discreetly, to tell stories and have a bonfire, and just be young and carefree. It was a break from the solemnity of their existence that

Letitia cherished. She looked forward to it every year and began counting down the days once the month of August was completed.

Tonight seemed the cause for special celebration. She had at last made the acquaintance of Charles Birch. He was the young man who had caught her eye and eagerly hoped to know better. He had hastened to her after meeting on Sunday, and had boldly come up to her on one side with Nathaniel on her other.

"Good day to you, Mistress Wood," he said as he swept off his hat and bowed deeply to her.

"Good day to you, sir," Letitia answered, a blush mounting her cheeks.

Her heart began to pound rapidly until it felt as if it were beating in her throat. She cast her eyes down nervously and her hands felt wet and clammy. She hoped that neither of the young men noticed how flustered she had become. She did not have to feign any traditional maidenly modesty, because Charles brought out every bit of it.

She looked up at him. He was tall; at least an inch or two over six feet. He had black curls that fell gracefully on his broad shoulders, and eyes the color of the waves that pounded the summer shore, blue-green with a hint of gray. His eyes shimmered brilliantly and she could see mischief lurking in their luminous depths. She sensed that here was one who knew how to enjoy life and brimmed over with high spirits that were not repressed like those of her neighbors. Immediately she felt a tug on her own heart, an answering call in her own spirit.

But none of this did she betray as she smiled and ducked her eyes once more from the brilliance of his gaze.

"I am Charles Birch," he continued. "I moved here from England recently with my father, who is the cousin of the aide of the new Governor of Boston who will be arriving shortly from England. We came to Massachusetts at the request of our good King William."

"King William?" Nathaniel interrupted, raising an eyebrow at the other young man as he did so.

It seemed to Letitia judging by the sparks that blazed in his dark eyes as he looked at the other young man and the way he tightened his lips that Nathaniel resented the interruption made by Charles Birch, and his subsequently taking Letitia's attention away from him.

"Indeed," Charles answered, and waited courteously for the other young man to continue.

"Well, you must find yourself at odds with this community," Nathaniel began, his breath coming in short gasps.

"And why is that, sir?" Charles asked as his lips curled and a twinkle shone in his dazzling eyes.

"A Puritan community, and you a King's man?" Nathaniel queried, talking over Letitia's head to the young man on her other side. "You must surely find yourself something of an outsider in Salem."

"Well, that may be true," Charles agreed, nodding his head slowly with a slight smile breaking across his face. "There do not seem to be very many people here cheering on the King. However, we are still the King's subjects here in Massachusetts.

"But whether I am an outsider or not, I must say that I thoroughly enjoy this community. I loved England and was saddened to leave it, having grown up there and leaving all of my friends behind; but I do find this to be a peaceful and lovely place, so unspoiled by progress brought on by advancing civilization. Indeed, one could say that it is somewhat bucolic, rather rustic, very refreshing, in fact!"

"Indeed, you *do*, sir," Nathaniel remarked dryly as he looked at Charles askance.

"Do what, sir?" Charles asked, with one eyebrow raised as he returned Nathan's glance.

"You say that it is rustic," Nathan said, as he frowned openly at Charles.

The conversation was growing noticeably strained and made Letitia uncomfortable. It was obvious that the two young men had nothing in common and that Nathaniel resented Charles intruding on his conversation with her. It was clear that his doing so announced his intentions to her, as they had not been formally introduced by a third party. For Charles to take the initiative was daring, and would brand him as a brazen young man from whom the village lasses should be guarded in the eyes of the community, Letitia knew.

It was also not lost on her that neither of the young men mentioned the name of King William's co-ruler, Queen Mary. It was unusual for man and wife to rule jointly, but for those who claimed that they had equal right to the throne it was a reasonable solution. That is, it was a reasonable solution in England and Europe, she thought; but here in this Puritan community the King was barely acknowledged, and his wife not at all.

"Sirs," she interjected, "perhaps we can find a more peaceful subject to discuss, something that will not cause dissension and discord among you. Please!"

And she beamed a winning smile upon both of them. Nathaniel and Charles both laughed albeit reluctantly, and to appease her bowed to one another but with barely suppressed hostility toward the other in their eyes.

This memory made her smile as she walked along with Constance to the village square. Yes, indeed, she did look forward to this evening.

She did not have very long to wait.

Charles spotted her at once and made for her side immediately like a bee hastening single-mindedly to a flower that seized its attention.

"May I have the pleasure of engaging you in the dance, Mistress Wood?" he asked with a smile that showed his flawless white teeth, bowing as he addressed her and flourishing his hat with its long plume as he did so.

The hat in itself marked him as an outsider, for Puritan men did not adorn theirs with any kind of trim. Their hats were conical with short brims, whereas Charles wore one with a wide brim adorned with a sweeping white plume. His black curls were at variance as well, contrasting with the closely cropped hair of the men of the village, who deemed curls to be a sign of vanity, only sported by men in more carnal societies.

His hat was a good match for her cream-colored cap with its green embroidery as an emblem for effrontery in the eyes of the villagers, Letitia thought.

But Letitia decided not to dwell on such differences this evening. Tonight was for pleasure and she intended to have some, and she felt a reckless joy seize her heart as she cast a dazzling smile upon the man who stood before her with an answering light in his own eyes.

"Indeed, you may, sir," she answered Charles, and prepared to give him her hand in the dance.

It was just at that moment that Nathaniel spied Letitia and walked over to join them.

"Ah, Mistress Wood," he addressed Letitia as he ignored Charles by her side, "may I have the honor of dancing with you?"

Letitia was suddenly flustered and felt her cheeks flaming, knowing that all eyes were upon the three of them, and seeing the young girls putting their heads together and whispering discreetly filled her with foreboding.

"Oh, I am so sorry," she panted, suddenly unable to breathe, "but Mr. Birch has already asked me and I have accepted."

Nathaniel's lips tightened and his brow furrowed in a scowl. But he remembered his manners and merely cast a tight little smile in Charles' direction and addressed Letitia.

"Well, then, perhaps you would grant me honor of the next dance?" he asked her, as he glared at Charles who smiled at him smugly as a smirk spread across his handsome features.

Letitia bowed her assent to Nathaniel and then turned to Charles, who took her by the hand and whisked her away as quickly as he could from the other young man.

They danced along merrily as they surrendered to the rhythm of the music, and laughed together with abandon to the tunes played on the fiddle, harp, and flute the songs the villagers enjoyed. After they ran out of breath they went to a booth where someone dispensed apples, berries, and roasted corn. They refreshed themselves with this fare and found a wooden bench set slightly apart from the crowd where they sat down to talk.

"Do you really like it here?" Letitia found the courage to ask him, for during the dance they had enjoyed each other's company so thoroughly and laughed so heartily that the ice was finally broken between them.

Charles paused for a moment to consider before answering. It appeared to Letitia that he was uncertain, and she found herself wondering why he hesitated. She was vaguely aware of the music still being played and the movements of those around her as she waited for Charles to speak.

"Yes, I do," he said at last. "It is very different from England, with the emphasis on rules and regulations and piety. Yet it is peaceful and serene, very lovely. But I do miss the variety of society in England, and I truly do feel like an outsider here, especially as I am loyal to the King.

"But it is a beautiful country. I enjoy walking on the beach and watching the waves come rolling in. I love the birds that descend on the ponds and the lakes. I delight in watching the wildlife, and savor the forests of pine and spruce with the aromas they disperse. It is indeed a lovely place, the kind that is rapidly beginning to disappear from the English countryside as the population grows larger."

"Oh, I love the beauty of it too," Letitia said. "But sometimes I feel like I don't really belong here, and yet I was born and raised in the village! I am different from the other girls, and they do not warm to me very much."

"I can see that," Charles chuckled.

"Why do you say that?" Letitia asked, suddenly defensive at the thought that someone was so quick to agree with her that she was different.

"Because all of the other maidens sit quietly looking at the minister as he preaches on the Sabbath day never moving, never stirring, sitting with their eyes straight ahead, like the good little girls they were raised to be. You, on the other hand, allow your eye to wander. You look out the window; you look around the room; you fidget with your hands; you twitch at your dress.

"It is clear that you are bored."

Charles smiled into her widened eyes at her shocked expression.

"And I like that," he added.

Suddenly he burst out laughing and Letitia found herself joining in his laughter. They laughed for several moments, finding it difficult to contain their hilarity. Charles wiped his eyes which were streaming with tears, and she laughed so hard she was afraid she would choke.

It was so good to finally find someone who saw things as she did.

Their merriment was suddenly interrupted by the sound of a scuffle and angry voices.

"Watch where you are going!" shrieked young Thomas Putnam.

He was addressing his remark to a couple who was blithely dancing by, and had accidentally stepped on his foot. Unfortunately, John Porter was one of the couple, and the bitter rivalry of the Putnams and Porters found a vent for their hostility. John Porter did not even address the angry young man; instead he acted. He drew back his arm and punched Thomas, knocking him off of his feet. A crowd quickly gathered around them as Thomas leaped back to his feet and hurled himself on John, and thrust him to the ground, where he proceeded to pummel him mercilessly.

At last Nathaniel intervened.

"Stop it; have done with this barbaric fighting!" he demanded, as he pulled John Porter off of Thomas Putnam.

Others in the crowd joined him, adding their voices to his.

The two young men glared at each other, and disregarding Nathaniel's injunction to shake hands, glared at one another and stalked off, anger erupting from every pore of their bodies. The crowd quickly dispersed and went back to their merrymaking. After all, the feud was one of long standing and would not be settled overnight; and how often did the young people have a chance to make merry?

Letitia felt a surge of admiration for Nathaniel and his courage in stepping between the fighting men to urge them to apologize. But a shiver ran down her spine as she looked at the retreating backs of the two young men who refused to make amends and live in peace as was required by every Christian believer according to the Holy Scriptures.

Chapter 7
Two of a Kind

From that night on their relationship flourished. They did not dare bring their attachment out in the open. Charles did not dare call upon her for he knew, he told her, that her parents did not approve of him. Indeed, it was evident and obvious to all who observed it that they were encouraging the courtship of Nathaniel to their daughter. And Nathaniel did not lag in this at all, but claimed a proprietary air upon Letitia, who frankly did not know what to do about the situation.

She posed the question to Constance one day as they met to walk together down to the stream to wash their family laundry.

"Tell me, Constance," she asked her friend, "what should I do about Nathaniel?"

Constance stiffened and blinked her eyes and turned abruptly to stare into Letitia's eyes and study her face.

"What do you mean?" she asked somewhat curtly.

Such behavior was foreign to Constance, who was always the soul of courtesy and gentleness, and it struck her as odd to Letitia, even as she hastened to explain what she meant by her question.

"It's clear that my parents are encouraging his attentions to me," she said, "and it is obvious that he is interested, although he has not called upon me yet. But I am not comfortable around him. I do not want him to court me, and I fear that is what he is doing."

Constance gasped as her jaw dropped suddenly. She shook her head slowly from side to side and stared unblinkingly at her friend.

"Have you taken leave of your senses?" she asked the other girl.

"What do you mean? Why do you say such a thing?" Letitia asked, as she laughed a little, albeit somewhat nervously.

"Because every girl in the village wants Nathaniel to court them; *every* one of them. And he is pursuing you and you don't *want* him? Are you out of your mind?"

Letitia stared at Constance for a moment, and considered her friend with a new flash of revelation.

"Do *you* want him to court *you*?" she asked.

Constance flushed a bright pink that was flattering to her fair complexion and blue eyes, and opened her mouth, only to shut it with an audible snap before attempting to answer. She cleared her throat and put a hand to her cap, smoothing back a few stray blond curls that escaped its confines, averting her gaze from Letitia as she did so.

"No," she said at last, "of course not."

She ducked her head and fiddled with the linen she was washing and half turned from her friend, apparently intent on doing the chore that she had set out to do.

But Letitia wondered...

"So what do I do?" she asked.

"You must decide that for yourself, Letitia," Constance answered. "No one can make

58

that decision for you."

Then she turned her head to the other girl and looked her fully in the face. Her eyes hardened as she did so, and her mouth tightened into a thin red line.

"But I would think that if you truly do *not* want him to call on you as you claim you do, that it is totally your decision and all you would have to do is to tell him that."

Letitia flinched at Constance's use of the word claim. But it was true that she did not want Nathanial to court her! Yet she had the impression that Constance doubted her word, and it troubled her that her friend did not believe her.

Letitia thought about her words for a moment. It was more customary among their people to arrange a marriage and make the decision for their offspring. Or if two young people did take a spontaneous liking to one another and it was a suitable match they allowed matters to run their course, which usually resulted in a marriage.

In this case, however, she was afraid to say anything. It was true, as Constance said that Nathaniel was the most sought after young man in the village. Letitia knew only too well the talk about him by the other girls, who giggled and speculated why he was still unmarried, and several had whispered with maidenly blushes that they wished he would notice them.

But what she was really afraid of was that her parents would find out that she was secretly sneaking away to meet Charles; along the lake, along the shore, in the woods, in any place they could find that was away from the prying eyes of the village. Because Charles was right; her parents would have been disapproving of him.

Charles had not been in the village for more than a few weeks before he had earned the disapproval of the townsfolk, and for nothing more than high spirits and frivolity. It was obvious to everyone who observed his behavior that he was as bored as Letitia during the Sunday meeting, and he would catch her eye and look at her and wink. She stifled a giggle and turned her face away from him stiffly to indicate disapproval of his manner. But yet he knew that she felt as he did, and he did not take offense. Nor did it stop him from trying to gain her attention more and more frequently.

One day after the meeting he paused and talked to her briefly. Before she realized what he was about he had slipped something into her hand and smiled into her eyes before hastening off. He bowed and left her, and when he had done so she walked a discreet distance away from the other villagers who were coming out of the Meeting House and examined what he had put in her hand.

It was a note.

"Meet me in the meadow by the old grove of trees this evening after you have completed your chores," the note said.

She blushed and became flustered, her hands started shaking so violently that the paper in her hand rustled, and her heart quickened its pace. She quickly thrust the note into the pocket of her gown and clenched her fists to stop their shaking. She drew deep breaths and exhaled slowly, gradually bringing the pace of her heart back to normal.

It was absolutely forbidden for a young maiden to meet a young man in secret. She knew that if anyone found out she would be open to scandal and gossip. Young girls could only meet suitors in the presence of a chaperone; in their homes, at dances, or village gatherings, but never alone.

And yet the temptation to meet him alone was irresistible. She fingered the note in her pocket and resolved in her heart to get away as soon as she could after the evening chores.

It was a beautiful night, the temperature warm for early October. There was a moon rising over the horizon, and the sun had started to set. The last of the summer crickets had begun their nightly song. A few lone fireflies were dancing around illuminating the darkness with tiny glows like candle light; soft, warm, and flickering.

Letitia walked to where Charles waited for her in the grove of trees. He gazed at her solemnly, and then held out his arm; she took it and smiled at him. They strolled along for several moments in complete silence. Yet it was not an awkward silence but one of complete and utter contentment, one of two souls that were so in agreement that they did not need to exchange words in order to make that fact known to each other.

The stillness continued for some time and then Letitia sighed as she looked up at the moon which was now full in the sky, silvery and shedding its soft radiance on the grass, turning it to gray in the moonlight, touching the gnarled old trunks of the trees in the grove and imbuing them with an unearthly aura. The first stars had emerged, popping out and looking like jewels surrounding the moon; yet they paled in comparison to its glory. A soft breeze ruffled the grass and touched Letitia's cheek as gently as a caress and she sighed once more, afraid to speak lest the spell of their harmony be broken.

"Why do you sigh?" Charles asked her in a murmur, as if he too were afraid to break the perfection of their tranquility.

"Because this is absolutely perfect," she breathed.

"What is perfect?" Charles asked her softly, looking at her with eyes that caressed her face.

"This," she said, "the moon, the stars, the soft breeze."

"And, anything else?" Charles asked her with a gleam in his eyes that revealed inward laughter. "Hmmm?"

She laughed softly.

"Oh, I *do* believe that there might be something more," she said as she smiled up into his eyes.

Charles suddenly took her hand and drew it to his lips. He kissed her hand softly, closing his eyes as he did so. When he opened his eyes and raised them to hers she saw the softness in his gaze and saw reflected there the same contentment that she felt. And she knew that he felt as she did; utterly and completely satisfied.

A few days later there was consternation in the village. The bell from the Meeting House was missing. It had been there in its usual place the night before but on the next day it was gone.

Distress quickly seized the townsfolk. How would the bell ringer call people to meeting on the Sabbath day without a bell?

Rumors spread quickly through the village.

"Someone has bewitched the steeple," it was said.

"Someone has been up to mischief," another muttered.

"We have a thief in our midst," said a third.

But this last statement was challenged by a rare citizen who exercised common sense.

"A thief?" someone asked. "What would someone want with a bell? Of what possible use could it be? What can you do with a bell except ring it?"

"I do not know," stammered the one who had made the statement.

"They stole it to annoy us," someone else was inspired to say.

"Yes!" said a third. "They don't want us to be able to come to meeting so the devil has put it in their heart to steal our bell."

"Well, we will show them," said one upstanding citizen. "We will come to meeting even without that bell. And we will have a good time too!"

"Yes, indeed we will," said another. "We will have a good time in spite of the devil's attempt to prevent our meeting."

When Letitia heard of the theft of the bell, a thought struck her immediately; then she negated it. He wouldn't. Would he?

But when the villagers went into the Meeting House on the Sabbath silently without the ringing of the bell on Sunday morning, she knew without a doubt by the nonchalant air and the whistle with which he had entered the room who the thief was that had stolen the bell. That suspicion was confirmed when Charles strolled in casually, sat down primly, and fastened his gaze upon the minister with only a hint of a smile lurking at the corners of his mouth.

Chapter 8
The Persistent Suitor

All of this did not escape the notice of everyone. There were those who were whispering that they knew very well, although they could not prove it, that somehow that young man from England had something to do with the theft of the bell. Why, he clearly did not respect their beliefs and frequently boasted of the connections his father had with the Governor of Massachusetts. But no one could prove that he had stolen it and so they fumed silently. Nor did anyone know what to think when the bell suddenly reappeared two weeks later back in its place.

The best solution, the villagers said, was to act as if nothing had happened, and therefore nothing was ever said.

It was at this time that Delilah shared with her older sister another mystery, one which would have graver and far more reaching consequences for Salem Village.

Delilah was two years older than Betty Parris, the daughter of the Reverend Parris, and with his niece Abigail Williams, who was exactly Delilah's age. Their mother Ruth approved of this friendship, for who could be better companions for her daughter than the daughter and niece of a man of the cloth? So absorbed was Letitia in her own affairs that she paid little heed to what happened in the life of her sister, for what could be so important about the events in the life of an eleven year old child?

Until Delilah sought her out one day to share a strange story, one that puzzled Letitia and would have repercussions for the village and all within it.

The Reverend Parris was tolerated in Salem Village as a man of the cloth, but not highly respected. He had difficulty with the quarreling populace, and was not successful in resolving the disputes that were occasionally brought to him to settle. It did not help that he was considered an outsider by those that he came to minister to and teach the ways of the Lord.

Samuel Parris was born in London into a family that was prosperous, although not wealthy. They owned a sugar plantation on the Caribbean island of Barbados, where Samuel took up his abode following the death of his father after being educated at Harvard University in Boston. It was on Barbados that he acquired two slaves, Native Indians named John and Tituba. Life on the island was very good, with perfect weather, pleasant neighbors, and want of any kind unknown, a virtual Eden to one who had known the gray skies and rainy climate of England. Until the day that a hurricane struck and destroyed much of his property, an occurrence that discouraged the Englishman, who simply did not know how to cope with such unpredictable catastrophes of a nature that was far different from the mild and steady climate of England, which he now greatly appreciated in the face of adversity.

Samuel sold some of his property and moved to Boston, which he had grown fond of during his University days and thought would be the perfect place to make a fresh start. There he met the beautiful Elizabeth Eldridge, whom he married and who bore him three children; Thomas, Elizabeth (known as Betty so as to be distinguished from her mother), and Susannah. They settled in Boston, although Samuel retained his interest in his sugar plantation, which still brought in revenue. After the hurricane that had caused such decimation of his property, he decided that it was folly to keep all of his eggs in one basket and searched for another and more steady source of income.

It was not clear to the citizens of Salem why he chose the ministry as an occupation. He did not seem in their opinion a man inclined to the spiritual, but rather, one who enjoyed the delights of the corporeal world. The townsfolk were shocked when he purchased gold candlesticks for their modest altar and new vessels for the sacraments. Such was viewed as worldly, extravagant, and an exhibition of pride; for was this not demonstrative of the very behavior that drove their ancestors from England to establish a country of their own?

Tension was further increased by the decision after a couple of years to stop paying the Reverend's wages. He was still granted use of the parsonage and the acreage it sat upon, but financial compensation was discontinued, an irony that perhaps only the Reverend himself could truly appreciate.

The village continued to employ him and

the Reverend ground out his sermons every Sunday morning; but his inability to connect with the townsfolk or resolve their disputes was a source of irritation that gnawed on the nerves of the man of God and citizens alike, one that would one day explode much as the earth occasionally does after plates underground pass each other warily until the day that one of them strikes another and releases a catastrophic event.

Delilah confided to Letitia that she was frightened.

"It is that slave woman, Tituba," she whispered one night in the bedchamber that they shared.

"What of her?" Letitia asked, curiosity succeeding in diverting her momentarily from her own problems.

Tituba was a strange woman, a Native Indian who exuded an exotic air, with her dress that was so different from the Puritan women. She wore long robes and a turban on her head and soft slippers on her feet. She lowered her eyes when she encountered the townsfolk in the village, but did not come to meeting. Such would have seemed inappropriate, to accompany her master to church. That her owner was also the town minister only complicated the situation, as there were some who questioned whether a minister had any business owning a slave. But these were in the minority, and they did not take issue with the Reverend over his ownership of slaves.

Letitia thought of these matters as Delilah

continued her story.

"Tituba practices magic," she said, "and tells us that she can reveal who our future husbands are. Betty and a few of her friends let her reveal that to them, and thought it was great fun. But Tituba also reads strange tales to us when I visit Betty and Abigail."

"What kind of tales?" Letitia inquired, as she felt a qualm of foreboding stir within her at her sister's words.

Delilah shuddered involuntarily, a fact that was not lost on her sister. Letitia's concern was now aroused. There had always been something strange about Tituba, and if she did anything to harm her sister...

"She tells us stories from a book about witchcraft," Delilah whispered.

"Witchcraft!" Letitia cried out, then quickly lowered her voice at her sister's urging.

"Shhh!" Delilah whispered. "You will wake Father and Mother."

Letitia nodded her head and bade her sister to continue.

"They are truly frightening tales, and disturb Betty and Abigail as well as they do me. They are all about witches and demons that consort with them, even visiting women in the night to, to," here Delilah blushed and hung her head.

Letitia could fill in the blanks. At sixteen she knew the facts of life, but felt it outrageous that her sister, who was little more than a child, should be exposed to such wickedness as this that the slave woman shared with the young girls. She knew that there were many in Salem

Village that believed in witches and demons, but she was appalled that children should be terrified with tales of them.

"I understand," Letitia hastened to assure the child.

Delilah shot her a relieved smile that spoke volumes of gratitude for sparing her embarrassment.

"What is the book that she reads to you from?" Letitia asked, intending to store up the information lest it become necessary to expose Tituba for frightening the little girls with her stories.

"She called it the Malleus Maleficarum," Delilah answered.

Letitia caught her breath in horror.

"She read to you from *that*!" she exclaimed.

It was a horrible book, Letitia knew, one that was infamous. Published more than two hundred years ago, it was considered the leading authority on witches and witchcraft, and had caused the destruction of thousands of people throughout Europe during the Burning Times. In those decades of horror, entire villages lay in danger of extermination through the trials of its citizens and the burning at the stake of those held to be guilty of witchcraft.

Whether or not they actually were was a question worthy of debate, as the definition of a witch had been altered greatly within its pages. For centuries a witch was regarded as one having magical powers granted to them by the worship of their gods. But in the Malleus Maleficarum, a witch was granted powers by the devil and subject to him through enslavement to his will, and in some cases, sexual relations with him or his demons. Such a definition incited fear in the Church, as it felt duty bound to stamp out any who were guilty of such relations with the devil or his minions, citing the need to take precaution against attacks on Christians through the agency of witchcraft empowered by the evil one himself.

The question in Letitia's mind, however, was where did the author obtain such information? Was it divine revelation from God as he claimed, or the fevered product of his own imagination? And while the Bible mentioned witchcraft and those who practiced magic, it was mysteriously silent on where those who practiced it obtained their powers; or if indeed they possessed any true power at all. One thing was certain in the content of its pages; and that was, that a true witch, one with proven powers to harm others, must not be permitted to live.

Letitia continued to escape at every moment that she could to meet with Charles secretly. The more frequently they met, the more they fell in love. Oh, how she looked forward to those meetings, those moments when she could bare her heart and speak with him about all of the things that perplexed her heart regarding her community, her family, and her feeling of being an outsider. Why, there were times when she felt that she did not even belong in her own family.

"I mean, listen, Charles," she said one

evening, "my mother's whole life revolves around cooking, cleaning, bringing up children, doing everything that father tells her. She has no other ambitions, or goals, or dreams. She is just a servant; a slave to his demands. She does his bidding at all times. What kind of an existence is that?"

"Well, that is not all that unusual," Charles stated. "Are not all young women brought up with that expectation? Are they not taught from childhood to be good wives, mothers, and housekeepers?"

"Yes! That is the problem," she cried.

"Why is that a problem?" he asked her with genuine puzzlement creasing his brow as he stared at her in bewilderment.

"Because I have dreams, too," she said with a moan in her voice. "I would love to go off on an adventure somewhere. Why, do you know that I have never been outside of my own village?"

"Never?" he asked, his voice rising in disbelief.

"Never. That is the way it is in this village. You can't travel very far; the roads are primitive and rough, and traveling is difficult; and even if you did manage to travel one village is very like another and so traveling becomes pointless, if you are seeking new horizons. One must go to a city such as Boston, which is only about fifteen miles away, but it's just too difficult to make the journey. I have never been outside of my own village. I would dearly love to travel on a ship and go to lands far away, the lands I have read of in books!"

And she sighed deeply as her frustration threatened to overwhelm her and cause her to sink into despair.

"Oh, there is nothing like travel," Charles agreed, as an eager light sprang into his sparkling eyes. "There is so much to explore in the world and it is a joy to see something new for the first time."

"Are you serious?" she asked him. "You have done this, traveled to far off lands?"

"Well, of course, I have," he answered her. "I came here from England, after all, quite a journey in itself. But even before then my father and I used to visit the mainland in Europe and we saw Holland and France and Germany."

"Oh, how wonderful!" Letitia exclaimed. "It must have been glorious!"

"Yes, it was," Charles agreed. "I met people with all kinds of backgrounds and who spoke in a variety of languages, some of them lilting and musical, some of them harsh and guttural, some of them that flowed with the beauty of poetry. They had all manner of customs that are quite different from our own. I tasted so many kinds of food, and learned so many traditions.

"Travel makes you appreciate the diversity of people. And yet God made all of us."

Letitia had a sudden memory of watching the waves on a sunny July day when she had accompanied her father to the port to meet a cargo ship pulling into harbor. The sun sparkled on them, making them look diamond studded, and her eyes were dazzled by the spectacle. The thought had come to her that the light touched and revealed the individual drops which were too many to count, yet together they made up one body of water. Thus it was with the Church, she thought; there were various denominations, yet one Body of believers. Or so it ought to be.

"Ah, I wish I could say the same for Salem," Letitia sighed. "But here, if you are not like everyone else they think there is something wrong with you. And I have been somewhat of an outsider all of my life, because I seem to keep shocking people, try though I might to fit in and be like everyone else. Constance is the only friend I have."

"Really?" he asked, as a frown marred his brow. "Only Constance?"

"What do you mean?" she asked him. "Do you doubt my word?"

"Oh, no," he hastened to assure her. "I do not doubt your word. But I would venture to say that you have more than just Constance for a friend."

"No; none of the other girls will really speak to me," she informed him. "They smile and say hello, and politely exchange a few words of no importance, and then they move on. I am deemed too different for them to bestow their friendship upon."

"It wasn't Constance I was thinking of," Charles said with a smile as he looked down at her and patted her hand.

Letitia knew exactly who he meant.

But she would not call Nathaniel a friend. In fact, Nathaniel was more of an irritation in her eyes. He still persisted in hanging around and waiting for her after meeting on Sunday and took her arm to stroll with her and exchange a few words with her; none of which had escaped the attention of the other villagers, most notably the young maidens who put their heads together and whispered.

And then one day he said the words she had dreaded to hear, and hoped to avoid hearing.

"I am going to call on you tonight, Mistress Wood," he said with a smile. "I have already been granted permission from your parents. Expect me about six o'clock this evening."

She had protested to her parents, but to no avail.

"I do not want Nathaniel to call on me!" she wailed to her mother.

Ruth tutted impatiently and momentarily stopped serving corn meal mush to her family to glance at her oldest daughter.

"Do not be foolish, Letitia," she said in the no nonsense tone of voice that Letitia always dreaded.

It was a tone that meant; I'll have no back talk from you, do as I say, and that is enough, the subject is closed.

"Nathaniel is a fine man and the most eligible in Salem Village. All of the maidens like him and you will do the same. If he is courting you, you will encourage him as any sensible maiden would."

"But," Letitia began to protest again, only to be interrupted by her father.

"That is enough, girl!" he barked. "You will do as your mother says."

Delilah shot her a commiserating glance, and smiled weakly at her older sister. Letitia was uncertain how much Delilah guessed of her relationship with Charles. She tried to be quiet when she sneaked out of their room to meet him in secret after nightfall, but it was possible that her sister woke in her absence and guessed the reason for it.

Six o'clock came and Letitia was fretting. In another hour she was due to have escaped to meet with Charles, but now she would have to put that off. She had sent him a signal after the meeting, the signal they had worked out with each other. She shook her head from side to side, indicating, "No, not tonight."

His face fell, but there was little that he could do. She had to do as her parents bade her to do. And right now they were ordering her to allow Nathaniel to call on her.

He came at six o'clock on the dot. She knew that he would be punctual. She just knew it. Everything Nathaniel did was perfect. Everything he did was right. Everything he did was in conformity with the standards, rules, and regulations of the Village of Salem.

Frequently Letitia hoped that he would do just one thing out of order, just one thing that went against the conformity of the villagers, so that she could find something wrong with him, some chink in his armor, some proof of his humanity in the perfection of his existence. But he never stepped out of line, never did anything unexpected, always said and did the right things, always attempted to please those around him.

"Mistress Wood," he addressed her as they sat before the fireplace, "I am so delighted to call upon you this evening."

They were alone in the room although her parents were still in the house, thus fulfilling their duty as chaperones. The chamber where they met was not large, with plain and sturdy furniture consisting of a settle, a rocking chair, two straight-backed chairs and a low stool. On the mantle over the fireplace was a snuffer for candles, two of which burned in the tall sconces of walnut wood that flanked the fireplace on the wall on either side of it. They lent a warm glow to the room and softened the austerity that was revealed in the full light of day.

"And I do hope that this is the first of many such evenings," he continued.

"And why is that, sir?" Letitia asked him coyly, determining in her heart that she was going to drive this man away, whether her parents liked it or not.

She was going to give him some subtle, and maybe some not so subtle hints of discouragement, of signals meant to tell him to leave her alone.

Nathaniel beamed on her warmly.

"I hope to call on you again because I find you a very commendable young woman whose acquaintance I would like to deepen. I would like to know you better, Mistress Wood."

"I cannot imagine why," she responded as she cast her eyes down and brushed her hand across her skirt.

This response caught him off guard and clearly surprised him. He started and blinked his eyes and fastened his gaze upon her.

"What kind of an answer is that, Mistress Wood?" he inquired as he continued his contemplation of her face.

Letitia smiled inwardly, pleased that she had succeeded in rattling his usually cool composure, and resolved to say as many shocking things as she dared in her determination to drive him away.

"Well, I am sure that there are other lasses in the village that are more attractive, more maidenly, and who have far more to offer than I do. In case it has escaped your notice, no one speaks to me much except my friend Constance. None of the other girls will even bother with me, except to exchange pleasantries. I really find it amazing that you have put yourself out to call upon and get to know a young woman who is clearly an outcast."

"Oh, I would not say that it is a matter of being an outcast," he chuckled. "You are far from being that, unlike Sarah Good who begs from her neighbors, or Sarah Osborne who refuses to come to meeting, claiming illness as an excuse, although three years is rather a long time to be ill. No, indeed," he said as he smiled at her reassuringly.

"Well, what else would you call it?" Letitia asked him.

Nathaniel looked at her for a long moment and a sudden and peculiar warmth sprang up into his eyes. To her astonishment Letitia found herself responding momentarily with a soft yielding that was almost tangible, leaning slightly toward him with a softening of her stiffened spine. He *was* indeed an attractive man. She found herself wishing she could like him; but she didn't.

"I would say that the other girls are jealous of you, but that does not make you an outcast," Nathaniel stated.

"Jealous!" Letitia exclaimed. "Of what would they be jealous? Why would anyone be jealous of *me*?"

"I would say it's possibly because you are attractive," Nathaniel said. "You are also different, you are unusual; and in the female mind it doesn't take more than that to invite the green eyed monster to make his presence known and make innuendos that are tantamount to accusation and justify rejection."

"I never saw it that way," she said, genuinely puzzled by this unexpected observation.

"But I am sure you are mistaken."

It did not stop there.

After he left on that first evening Letitia told her mother when asked what she thought of Nathaniel, that she wished she could see something human in him.

"Whatever do you mean, Letitia?" her mother cried. "Nathaniel is a fine young man and any young woman in this village would be more than pleased to engage his attention and encourage his courtship. Why would my daughter be any different?"

"Because he never does anything wrong,"

Letitia answered. "He is dependable, upright, and unfailingly consistent. He is *boring.*"

"Boring!" her mother exclaimed. "He is the most eligible bachelor in Salem Village. And I will not allow any daughter of mine to discourage his attention. In fact, I forbid it. If he continues to want to call upon you, you will allow him to pursue you, young lady. And I mean it."

Nathaniel did not need the encouragement from Letitia's mother to continue calling on her. If he sensed hostility or reluctance on Letitia's part he chose to ignore it. His calls became a weekly ritual, one that Letitia dreaded every week.

Every Sunday evening he came to call. Every Sunday evening he brought some little gift. He brought a little box that he had carved from cedar wood in which she could place buttons, pins, or needles. He brought a fine pelt that he had bartered from some Indians that was warm and could be used as a covering on a cold winter night.

He even brought her a book of sonnets, written by some of the finest of English poets that he had purchased on a recent visit to Boston. This she did enjoy, and she found herself warming to Nathaniel through this gift, seeing in him an unexpected flash of culture and refinement, of a love of beauty and music that evoked a response in her.

Indeed, Nathaniel had a fine singing voice, and one night he treated her to listening to it. He brought with him a lute that he had also purchased in Boston (the playing of musical instruments being frowned upon by the Puritans of Salem) and played and sang a lovely song written by the English poet-priest John Donne.

Nathaniel also read one of Donne's Meditations aloud, and Letitia found haunting the lines that ended, "any mans death diminishes me, because I am involved in Mankinde; and therefore never send to know for whom the bell tolls; it tolls for thee."

As she listened Letitia discovered that she enjoyed Nathaniel's company, and found his voice lovely and his playing on the lute skilled. She responded at last to the warmth of his voice, the tenderness in his dark eyes when he gazed at her. And she melted under that gaze for the first time.

And that evening when he said goodnight and bowed over her hand, she found herself holding her hand in mid-air after he left, looking after him silently, and wondered when he might come to see her again.

Chapter 9
Dreams and Divinations

"I just do not know what to do," Letitia whispered to Constance one day as they met at the stream to do the daily washing.

The November days were growing colder, and the girls did not linger over their task, finding the chill of autumn fully descending on them, and the water of the stream icy cold as it tumbled over the rocks where they scrubbed the linens.

"What do you mean?" Constance asked her.

There was a new coolness in Constance's manner toward her but Letitia shrugged it off. So involved was she in the quandary that faced her that she failed to notice any change in her friend's behavior.

"I do not know what to do about Nathaniel," she said.

"Again? You are bringing that up *again*? You are allowing him to call upon you every week," Constance remarked and looked at Letitia wonderingly, clearly puzzled at her friend's behavior. "How can you say that you still do not know what to do about him?"

"I know!" Letitia exclaimed. "But I am just not sure of what to do. I only wish that I did!"

Constance sighed deeply and shook her head so fiercely that her cap loosened on her head and she had to take the time to secure it back into place. She stood up quickly and brushed blades of grass from her skirt. She did not look at Letitia as she spoke.

"Letitia, you are a mystery."

"Oh, I wish I were not," Letitia sighed in turn. "I wish I were like everyone else but I am not. And I have never known what to do about it."

"Well, you are a good person," Constance relented as she assured her. "Do not worry about it. You must go with what is in your heart. If you do not love Nathaniel, then don't marry him. Do not allow anyone to talk you into it, not even your parents, even if they insist on it."

"But my mother is practically ordaining it," Letitia informed Constance.

She sighed in frustration and kicked at a loose stone in the path after they had gathered their laundry and headed back to their homes.

"Well, it's not your mother's life," Constance said. "You alone determine your fate and the course of your life."

"Oh, that is *not* a good answer to give me," Letitia declared as she kicked another stone with greater force this time.

"What do you mean?" Constance asked, as she turned to look at her friend, her brow furrowed and the expression in her eyes clearly revealed her puzzlement at the other girl's statement.

"What I mean," Letitia answered, "is that every good girl is supposed to do whatever her mother or father tells her. You know that is what we have always been taught. Therefore, if Nathaniel asks me to marry him, I am supposed to accept. Isn't that what every good little girl is supposed to do?"

"Oh, I understand what you mean," Constance replied, and turned her eyes back to the path under her feet as they continued their walk. "Well, I would ordinarily agree with you and say yes. But you are the one who is going to have to live with your decision for the rest of your life. And if you have such an aversion to Nathaniel as that, what good can it do anyone if you say yes when he asks you?"

"That's what I mean," Letitia sighed as she kicked at another loose stone in the path so violently that it struck a rock on the side of the path and shattered in two.

Constance sighed also and linked her arm through Letitia's as they continued their walk homeward in silence.

Letitia truly did not know what to do about her predicament. She was entertaining Nathaniel on Sunday evenings when he came to call and allowing him to escort her into the Meeting House on Sunday mornings, but still meeting Charles in secret every chance that she could find. And the more that she and Charles met the more frustrated she became, and he became as well.

"Oh, when can we meet openly?" he asked her one evening.

"I wish that we could," she moaned.

"And when are you going to stop seeing Nathaniel?" he asked.

"Well, I don't know what to do about that," she cried. "My parents are insisting that I allow him to court me."

"Yes, but is it fair to him to allow him to

do so when you are meeting me in secret?" he inquired. "What kind of a courtship is that? You're encouraging him. You're leading him on. And no man likes that!"

"But I don't know what to do!" she exclaimed.

Charles ruffled her hair and kissed her brow. He had never kissed her; it would have been considered scandalous to allow him to do so. The most she could let him do in the way of caresses was to kiss her hand and look at her longingly. But sometimes she wondered what a kiss would be like. She thought of it as possibly the sweetest moment she would ever know; her first kiss. And she longed for it to happen.

But she had another dilemma that perplexed her; this one was even more unexpected and even harder to resolve.

As much as she was in love with Charles, she found herself warming to Nathaniel when he was around her. It was hard to resist such a persistent wooer. For he had truly fallen for her; she could see it in the way he looked at her with tenderness in his eyes, the warmth in his voice when he spoke her name and how he lingered on it when he said it, the way the light leaped into his eyes when he spotted her on Sunday morning as he waited on the steps of the Meeting House waiting to escort her in.

How could she possibly tell such a man no? And when everyone was expecting an announcement to be made; and no one knew that she met her lover in secret. It was a dilemma that was rapidly becoming an obsessive quandary that threatened to overwhelm her into a morass of despair.

And then one night she had a dream.

She dreamed she was standing in a field in the moonlight. There before her were two trees. One tree stood tall and upright without any break in its perfect symmetry; it seemed to reach to the very heavens. It was gray but touched with silver in the moonlight and shorn of leaves, just a stark outline of majesty silhouetted against the sky.

The other tree was broad and had heavy foliage on it, so heavy that you could climb into that tree and hide from the view of all. And you could hide and be safe from all things, from anything that moved on the ground. And yet it was mysterious; indeed, it was shady. She stood between the two, unable to decide which tree she should ascend, which one to climb, which one to choose.

When she woke up she was sweating so profusely that her hair was matted together in wet clumps of curls. Her skin felt cold and her heart was pounding. Then she realized that the trees in her dream were her two suitors; Nathaniel so upright, so solid and respectable with nothing to hide, his life an open book, his character honest and commendable. And the other tree was Charles, the one she met in secret, the one who was an outsider just as she was.

And she did not know how to solve this dilemma.

One day as she finished washing the

family linen she headed back to her home. Constance had not come today and Letitia had not waited for her, as she had a lot of chores to do before she could escape and meet Charles. As she walked along she met the slave woman, Tituba, who was bound on an errand for her mistress.

"Good day to you, Mistress Wood," said Tituba.

"Good day to you, Tituba," Letitia answered.

She bowed politely as she addressed the slave woman. She tried to hide it, but there was something about Tituba that made her extremely uncomfortable. She knew that she was from the West Indies and it was rumored by some of the villagers that she practiced black magic and knew the arts of witchcraft and divination. Some would have said it was just fortune telling done for entertainment, but others said she engaged in deeper occult practices than that and was in league with the devil himself.

According to her sister Delilah, Tituba practiced some divination in a seemingly innocent way, yet frightened the little girls with tales of witchcraft, but from what motive Letitia did not know. Was it to frighten them away from witchcraft, giving them a bizarre warning of what happened to those who practiced it? Or did she do it from a more sinister motive, the least of which was to inflict terror in the little girls of her master's household as some kind of warped revenge for the loss of her freedom? Delilah had since informed Letitia that Betty and Abigail were increasingly frightened of witchcraft and feared that it might lurk in their midst, thanks to Tituba's terrifying tales that she read to them from the Malleus Maleficarum.

Letitia did not know what to believe, as she did not really know the woman. Tituba, however, was smiling at her warmly, her face glowing with the sincerity of friendliness in her warm brown eyes, and it struck Letitia that the woman was lonely and enjoyed interaction with other villagers.

And suddenly Letitia had a thought.

No! She couldn't, she thought to herself.

Yes, the whisper tantalized her. Do it, ask her; no one will ever know. No one knows about you and Charles; no one will know about this. And besides; did she not have a duty to find out exactly what kind of divination her sister and the other little girls had been exposed to by the slave woman?

Did she not have an obligation to ascertain whether they had been harmed in any way?

The next evening Letitia made her way to the Reverend Parris' house where Tituba was a servant. She waited until she was certain that the minister and the rest of the household was abed for the night, knowing from her sister that they retired early, and that Tituba continued her chores for some time after that. Letitia then knocked discreetly at the back door.

"Tituba," she whispered. "Come, I need to speak with you."

Tituba peered out the window, saw the young girl and hastened out the door, wiping her hands on her apron as she did so. She had just finished tidying the kitchen and was just putting the house to rights when she heard Letitia's soft knock.

"Come," Letitia said, motioning for the slave woman to join her in the woods where she was heading. "I have something to ask you."

"What is it?" Tituba inquired, once they were safely out of sight in the trees.

Letitia hesitated. She knew that she was taking a big step, indeed, that she was exposing herself to strange and mysterious powers if Tituba had any authentic ones of her own. She also knew that she risked incurring the wrath of God for seeking out a diviner, if such Tituba proved to be.

And yet her desperation drove her to this drastic measure.

"Is there any way of knowing who my future husband will be?"

"Ha, ha; nothing simpler," Tituba laughed.

"How can I do it? Can you tell me how?" Letitia asked.

"I can show you..."

"No!" Letitia interrupted. "I cannot be seen consulting you. Please, I must be very careful not to upset my parents. But if you tell me how to do it, I think I can do it on my own. Just tell me how to do such a thing."

"Well, it's like this," Tituba lowered her voice and whispered.

Letitia listened to her intently, nodding her head as she listened, and walked away from her as Tituba made her way back to the Reverend's house.

As she crept along the line of the woods to return to her home, Letitia heard other steps that seemed to echo her own. She whirled around in fright; but saw no one. She strained her eyes to see into the dark woods; they revealed nothing.

After her parents retired for the night Letitia stole into the kitchen and took a cup from the cupboard that she took out to the small stream that flowed behind the house. She filled it with the water that tumbled over the rocks in the stream and then she went to the cooling house and selected an egg which she broke open and strained the yolk from, careful to save the white, which she dumped into the water.

She trembled and waited for it to happen. And then she saw it; she saw the shape of a profile form that, according to Tituba, was of the man that she would one day marry.

"Oh, my," she breathed, but she could not make out clearly yet whose profile it was.

Suddenly a breeze blew up and skimmed across the surface of the water in the cup, distorting the image. And it was dissipated and faded into nothingness, and was lost forever.

Chapter 10
Whispers

"There she is!" Remembrance whispered into the ears of Chastity.

Letitia heard her as she walked down the lane toward the stream to do the washing for the day. She greeted them but they averted their eyes from her and then whispered openly, but not audibly enough that she could hear what they were saying.

Well, that was rude, she thought to herself. Surely they were brought up with better manners than that!

She tried to pretend that she didn't notice, and kept her eyes averted from them. Nevertheless, she felt a lump in her throat and the sting of tears behind her eyes. Without warning she felt a surge of anger rise up within her. What had she done to merit such rude treatment? She had always been friendly to all of the villagers, and honestly wished to be on friendlier terms with the other maidens, who usually were courteous if not always very cordial.

But the behavior of Remembrance and Chastity and their rudeness toward her was unlike any treatment she had ever received before.

She could not believe they would actually whisper about someone in their presence like that. She would truthfully not be surprised if they were talking about her behind her back, as she had never been popular with the other girls.

But for them to openly talk about her in front of her? She found this somewhat disturbing and wondered what such behavior was about.

She walked on ahead of Remembrance and Chastity and continued on down to the stream where she took out the linens she had brought to wash for her family. She greeted Prudence and Humility who were already at the stream but suddenly the two girls moved away from her. Without a word of greeting they gathered their laundry and left the stream to her alone. Letitia looked after them wondering what was happening. Why was she suddenly being whispered about and left alone like this?

She felt alone and afraid suddenly as fear came over her and threatened to engulf her. She felt as if a dark cloud had appeared over her head and blocked the sunlight, bringing with it the threat of a storm about to break.

What is going on, she wondered. Why am I suddenly being shunned?

She proceeded with her washing, but with uneasiness growing in her heart as she pondered on the strange behavior of the other girls.

Shortly afterward Constance came to the stream.

"Good day, Letitia," she said rather jauntily as she bounced along, a smile lurking in the corners of her mouth.

"Hello, Constance," Letitia said, still preoccupied with the strange behavior of the other girls.

They washed their linens and did not

speak for several minutes, Constance humming a little tune under her breath and Letitia puzzling over the earlier incident and wondering what had precipitated it.

Suddenly she decided to ask her friend a question.

"Tell me, Constance, what is going on?

"Why, I do not know what you mean, Letitia," Constance answered as she looked blankly at the other girl. "Please explain yourself."

Constance dipped a sheet into the cold water tumbling over the rocks as she spoke. She continued humming her little tune and scrubbed the sheet against the rocks, removed it, and prepared to do the rest of the washing, waiting for her friend to speak as she did so.

Yet she did not look at Letitia, which Letitia found rather odd.

"Constance, I was heading here to wash my clothes and I passed Remembrance and Chastity. I told them hello, but they didn't speak to me. Instead they started whispering, right in front of me, to each other! And then when I arrived here I saw Prudence and Humility and greeted them. They said nothing to me and moved away from me and left me alone at the stream. Something is going on. Tell me what it is, if you have any inkling of it."

"Why, I have no idea," Constance said. "I do not know of anything that is happening. But you have never really been liked, Letitia."

Letitia gasped and felt a sharp pain in her abdomen as if she had fallen on her stomach and had the wind knocked out of her.

"Is that the way it is?" she asked Constance. "Just that bluntly, that forthrightly, I am not *liked*?"

"Well," Constance hastened to assure her, "I wouldn't say it's quite like that. I wouldn't say you are disliked exactly; you're just not accepted. But you already know that. You're different."

"Yes, I *am* different," Letitia huffed, beginning to draw her body up erectly with an attempt at dignity. "I actually think for myself. I actually question what the minister says. I actually question whether his view of God is based on the way He is portrayed in the Bible, or the way He is portrayed only in the minister's mind."

Constance's eyes widened in her face but Letitia found herself venting the years of frustration and would not be quiet.

"I question some of the teachings of Cotton Mather that he writes of in his pamphlets. I question some of the customs we Puritans have handed down for generations, believing them because our forefathers did. I question whether some of them are made up just to keep us in line."

"Made up?" Constance challenged. "No one has made anything up. It's an interpretation of Scripture we have, Letitia. You know that. And no one else has that insight as we do."

She tilted her head and lifted her chin and smiled rather smugly at her friend, almost smirking, Letitia thought in shock.

Did she really know Constance? Had she always been like this? Smug, arrogant, knowing it all? This was a new side of her friend that she was not aware of. And she wasn't certain that she liked it.

Within a few days Letitia was certain that she was not imagining things. When she went to the Meeting House that Sunday morning Nathaniel alone stood to greet her. When she sat down to join the other maidens they moved as far away from her as possible, even as the girls at the stream had done. She found herself with a pew all to herself, because the others who had been sitting on it got up and walked away as soon as she sat down on it.

Tears sprang to her eyes, and her face grew red, and she felt an unbearable tightness in her chest, almost as if her heart would burst out of it. She felt humiliated, and although she did not why it was so she was clearly being shunned, and for a reason she did not know of. She wondered again what was happening. Why was she being shunned?

She could not focus on anything the Reverend Parris said that morning and could not meet the eyes of Charles, so great was her embarrassment. She wished that the floor would open up and swallow her so that she could hide from the disgrace of her rejection by the other girls.

Nathaniel waited faithfully for her after the meeting, escorted her down the steps, and told her that he would call upon her that evening as usual. For once she found herself looking forward to it. At least there was someone in this town that was still speaking to her.

Letitia suffered silently. She did not mention the shunning to her parents. She did her chores dutifully and without flinching, but she longed to escape to solitude to think and sort things out.

After the morning chores were done, and she had swept the floors, washed up the breakfast dishes, made the beds, and washed the linens at the stream, she found her opportunity for escape. With a hasty word to her mother telling her the time of her return, Letitia scurried to the woods, now brilliant with the jewel-like colors of autumn. She walked briskly on the path, now lined with gold, brown, purple, and scarlet leaves lit with an unearthly brilliance by the rays of the morning sun, until she came to the stream.

Here the maples were aflame, and their crimson glory was reflected in the stream where they lined the banks. One particular tree had low-lying branches that draped over the stream, and as the cool breeze blew through the tree it rustled the branches, making their reflection waver in the water below, catching the sunlight and making the leaves sparkle like rubies in the river.

Letitia felt peace flood into her soul and her agitation stilled. She scrambled down to the bank and sat beneath the maple, its branches encompassing her, feeling its leaves caress her cheek when the wind ruffled them. She brought her knees up and laid her head down on them, and listened to the wind in the trees and the lapping of the water against the riverbank.

It came to her suddenly how much wind affected life. It could carry seeds on its currents to be planted elsewhere in the forest, or it could send waves crashing onto the shores to threaten the structures erected by man. Here under the maple branches and leaning against the trunk, however, Letitia did not feel cold, although the wind was brisk. She was sheltered by the trunk at her back and the branches that draped down around her.

A revelation came to her that the red branches that insulated her from the wind and kept her warm was rather like the scarlet cord that protected Rahab the harlot and her family in the raid on Jericho. Or like the blood that the Israelites applied over their doors when the destroying angel passed through Egypt. When it saw the red the angel passed over...

That is rather like the blood of Christ, Letitia thought. It covers us, protects us, and shelters us from all harm. No power of evil can defeat it, because the blood defeated the power of sin and darkness.

This thought gave her encouragement. Surely her God would look after her and protect her from all evil. For had she not given her heart into His keeping, and sought Him with all of her soul?

Letitia rose to her feet thoughtfully and walked slowly back to her home, where the task of helping her mother prepare the evening meal waited for her.

On Sunday Letitia was once again

shunned by the maidens of the village when she entered the Meeting House. Nathaniel greeted her with his usual friendly smile, and whispered in her ear that he would call at the usual time. She smiled her thanks and allowed him to escort her to a seat. But the other girls hurried away from her as they had done the previous week and avoided looking at her, and their coldness sent a chill into Letitia's heart, and she took her seat with shivers suddenly racking her body and her teeth chattering in apprehension.

"Constance, I need to speak to you," Letitia insisted one day as they met at the stream to do the daily washing.

Constance sighed and rolled her eyes with barely concealed impatience.

"Are we going to go through that again about Nathaniel?" she asked.

"No, we are not going to go through that again about Nathaniel," Letitia said with urgency in her tone. "I need to know what is being said about me."

"I do not know what you mean," Constance said firmly.

But she avoided Letitia's eyes and her friend did not believe her. She grabbed the other girl's arm and turned her about to face her.

"Nonsense! You know everybody, you are friends with everyone. Surely you must know that there is something being said about me. People will not even sit with me at meeting anymore. No one is speaking to me, and I don't know why."

"Well, you still have *Nathaniel* speaking to

you. Surely that is all you need," Constance snapped at her and then closed her mouth quickly. "I am sorry, Letitia. I did not mean to be rude."

"But you *were* rude; that was very rude," Letitia said. "Yes, Nathaniel is still speaking to me and I am very grateful that he is."

"And I am still speaking to you," Constance said.

"Yes, you are still speaking to me," Letitia agreed as she softened her voice. "Truly I am grateful for your friendship and I always have been. And I always will be."

Constance smiled at her sweetly with the pure radiance that, in Letitia's opinion bespoke a clear conscience and an innocent heart.

"Yes, we still are friends," Constance stated.

Letitia smiled gratefully at her in return.

"And that is why I expect you to tell me why people are shunning me."

Constance closed her eyes and sighed, her shoulders sagging as she did so. It was several moments before she answered Letitia, moments in which it was obvious that she struggled for patience.

"In truth, I really do not know," Constance stated in a dull monotone. "Do you have some secret that no one was aware of and somebody found it out and revealed it?"

Letitia flushed uncomfortably and cast her eyes down away from Constance's boring gaze. She suddenly could not bear to meet her friend's eyes. Yes, indeed, she *did* have a secret that no one was aware of, and that was her meetings with Charles. And no one must ever be aware of that.

Was it possible? Was it possible that someone spotted them together and her reputation was suddenly blemished? Did that account for the whispers, the shunning by the other maidens of the village?

It made sense, she thought. But who would know about it? Who could possibly be aware of it?

And then something occurred to her. She had a flash of memory. Going secretly to the parsonage to seek out Tituba and asking her whom she would marry.

If there was anyone who might be aware that she was seeing another man while encouraging the courtship of Nathaniel, it would be Tituba; Tituba, who had the gift of divination, and who probably knew the secrets of her heart. She probably was fully aware that she was meeting a man in secret, something that was totally contrary to the customs of her people, and forbidden to all young Puritan maidens.

Chapter 11
Outbreak of Accusations

It was the storm that had been brewing for some time; whispers, innuendos; it had been far too quiet. Letitia sometimes thought that it was the calm before the storm, as her father was fond of saying, right before one of the hurricanes or nor'easters borne in from the Atlantic came roaring through New England on a sultry summer day. The heat had been building as thunder lurked on the horizon while towering clouds massed overhead.

It felt like that right now. She had a sense of storm clouds gathering, waiting to break. The silence was ominous, carrying with it a hidden threat, just waiting for a strike of lightning to set the countryside aflame.

She would walk into the Meeting House and all voices would cease; no one would speak to her. She stopped going to the young people's gatherings because no one said a word to her. Only Nathaniel continued to call upon her; only Constance of the young girls of the village continued to speak to her.

And Charles still met her secretly, although over the winter it was more difficult and they met less frequently. Indeed, at times the snow was too deep for either of them to venture forth, and they had to be satisfied with secret signals and meeting on the outskirts of the woods for just a brief rendezvous before the cold drove Letitia back indoors.

And yet, she felt secure in his love. She

was affirmed that it was steadfast, firm, and unwavering. But as he saw how she continued to be shunned in the village and became more and more of an outcast, Charles grew increasingly concerned. He had been in the village long enough now to become aware of how the townsfolk treated outcasts, and apprehension grew within him as he witnessed the treatment doled out to his beloved.

And Letitia found herself looking over her shoulder fearfully, wondering with dread in her heart what would happen next.

The storm broke with such intensity that the village never recovered from it; never again in its history would it be the same.

It was February. The winter had dragged on, and the villagers looked forward to the coming of spring. Many had fallen ill over the cold months and been housebound until the advent of warmer weather.

It was at this time that the daughter of the Reverend Parris suddenly began acting peculiar. The girl appeared to throw herself around in tantrums and fits, claiming that she saw specters and visions. She said that she saw people that were not in the room and cowed in fright at their appearance.

The Reverend was greatly concerned, especially as Betty's cousin Abigail Williams claimed that she saw the same visions as Betty did, and soon began to exhibit the same behavior. They screamed with ear-piercing intensity, threw objects around the room, and crawled under furniture where they made peculiar sounds that were unearthly, high-pitched wails that sounded like the screams of a banshee, or the barking of a dog. They insisted someone that no one could see was pricking them with needles; they felt pain in their arms and legs that made them jerk as they cried out in agony.

Soon there were other young girls in Salem Village that exhibited the same bizarre behavior; Elizabeth Hubbard, Ann Putnam Jr., her best friend Mary Walcott, and Mercy Lewis, who was a servant in the Putnam household. All of the girls exhibited the strange behavior that had afflicted those in the parsonage.

The Reverend Parris fought a sense of rising panic as he witnessed the increasingly strange and frightening behavior of these girls, who were ordinarily quiet and sedate in their manner.

He felt so helpless in the face of this strange affliction that had beset the girls that he had called in two other ministers for assistance; the Reverend John Hale from the town of Beverly, and Reverend Deodat Lawson, who had preceded him in the pulpit at Salem Village.

Both of these men witnessed the peculiar behavior of the girls and were at a loss for explanation.

"Look at that!" Reverend Hale exclaimed in a whisper, as though afraid to speak out loud.

Reverend Parris and Reverend Lawson followed his pointing finger. The girls appeared to have been bitten by an invisible tormenter, and they jerked their bodies violently from side to side and back and forth in ways that seemed beyond the ability of a human to execute.

"How do you explain this?" asked Reverend Lawson in a hollow voice, who had never seen such a thing or even dreamed of it before.

Reverend Parris had heard of such things when he lived in Barbados, but kept his fears to himself. But it was left to the Reverend Hale to articulate his fear and put it into words.

"I fear that the children have done something or been exposed to something that has opened the door to demonic possession of some sort," he said slowly in a voice that trembled slightly.

He glanced at the Reverend Parris with wide eyes, and saw that the Reverend Parris was pale, with beads of sweat dotting his brows. He licked his lips slightly and cleared his throat.

"Stop it! Stop it!" the girls screamed, as their eyes bulged so greatly in terror that they looked as though they would pop out of their heads.

"Whom are you speaking to?" the Reverend Parris demanded, his voice roughened with fear, even as he strived to remain calm and appear in control of the situation.

"The witch, witch; the witch that's doing this to us!" they all declared, all of them in chorus, all of them in unison with one voice.

"Yes, she is sticking us with pins, torturing us! Make her stop it!" Abigail screamed in agony.

In this she was joined by her cousin Betty, and from the other household, Ann, Mary, and

Mercy, who also accused an invisible tormentor of sticking them with pins.

Doctor William Griggs was brought in to give each of the girls a physical examination; but he could find no evidence of any ailment. Unlike Reverend Hale, he claimed that he did not see any marks on their bodies that would account for the pain they suffered.

As he left the room where he had examined the girls, now quarantined at the parsonage, he shook his head and addressed the Reverend Parris.

"I am sorry, but I do not find anything wrong with any of them," he sighed heavily. "All of these histrionics and dramas...may just be the imagination of preadolescent girls."

Mistress Elizabeth Parris protested when he made this statement.

"My daughter would *never* tell a lie," she huffed, as she glared at the doctor. "And it is doubtful that Abigail would either, as they were raised together. If they say they are being tortured, then they are indeed being tortured."

Doctor Griggs lifted one eyebrow at Mistress Parris and shook his head as he looked at her with pitying eyes.

"Forgive me, lady, but there is no evidence to support their claims, and so I must come to the conclusion that all of these scenes and tantrums are merely the overactive imaginations of little girls."

Elizabeth Parris looked at the doctor as if he were something that the family dog had dug up and brought into her nice clean home without permission, and turned to her husband for support.

"Samuel," she began.

The Reverend did not hesitate.

"If my wife is certain that the girls are telling the truth, then they must be telling the truth. For who would know them better than she who raised them? And she brought them up to be modest, honest, God-fearing young ladies. They would not deliberately tell a lie."

"But witchcraft?" the doctor inquired, as he looked askance at Elizabeth.

"Well, and why not?" Elizabeth challenged as she withered him with her eyes. "What other explanation could there be? All know that the devil roams around seeking whom he may devour; why wouldn't he prey on innocent children who cannot defend themselves from his attack?"

Doctor Griggs sighed and took his leave. The Parris' did not bid him good-day as he left, nor did they invite him under their roof again.

The strange behavior of the young girls continued, and became the talk of Salem Village. They screamed, cried out, jerked their bodies around, and insisted they were being tormented by invisible hands. All of them stuck to their story as they sang the same tune, stating that they were the victims of witchcraft.

No one knew what to say or think in light of their strange and frightening behavior. Those who witnessed it and heard their screams said it made the hairs on the nape of their neck stand up, so eerie was the sound. Clearly there was something wrong; all of the girls had previously always been quiet, modest, calm, the very embodiment of maidenly virtue and propriety. And Betty Parris and Abigail Williams had always been respectable and well-behaved, as befitted the daughter and niece of a minister. Truly they exemplified the virtues of young women whose father and uncle was a man of the cloth. So what had caused this strange behavior?

The murmuring began, and then the murmuring grew into lowered voices, and then it became a grumble, and then it became a cry, a howl of accusation.

"Witchcraft! Witchcraft! There is a witch in our midst! Find her; find her!"

The townspeople panicked. It was not long before the accusations flew; it was not long before the arrests began. It began with Sarah Osborne, Sarah Good, and Tituba early in the month of March.

Tituba, it was said, had read excerpts from the Malleus Maleficarum to the girls, entertaining them with stories of witchcraft, of seductive spirits, of evil perpetrated long ago that had been handed down through the ages; of occult mysteries secretly performed since the dawn of time, known only to the few initiated into the covert rites, only to those that were blessed by the devil. She had also led these young innocents into participating in occult practices, telling their fortunes, and inciting them to seek out evil. For this the girls were forgiven, being mere children, but Tituba must be punished for attempting to teach the girls the devil's ways.

Sarah Good, as everyone knew, was an outcast. She did not come to meeting; and she lived on the outskirts of Salem Village in the surrounding woods. She had lost everything she possessed in trying to settle the debts left by her first husband and was reduced to begging her neighbors for food or work for payment, so that she could buy clothing for her daughter. Her husband William did little to help her, it was said, and frequently referred to his wife as a witch because she lost her temper so easily. She had stepped on the toes of her neighbors far too often, being accused of cursing their cattle and casting enchantments upon them if they refused to give their aid.

It was easy to accuse such a one, as she had no one to defend her.

Sarah Osborne was a more respectable member of the community, and yet accusations were made against her as well. For one thing, she had not attended meeting in more than three years. That she suffered ill health was deemed no excuse, said the townsfolk. All should attend meeting, whether they were ill or well, and she was no exception.

Letitia was stunned when she heard all of the rumors coming through the village, and all of the stories. Indeed, she was terrified. If Sarah Good could be arrested simply because of being an outcast, then what of her, to whom no one was speaking and everyone was shunning, just as they did Sarah Good?

And Tituba! She had secretly consulted Tituba; what if that were made known? What if someone found out? What if she too were accused?

The terror began to grow. The villagers, day by day, had their hysteria multiplied as they heard one story after the other, each one increasing the terror in which they walked.

How could such innocent people, or at least people that they had previously thought innocent, and who seemed so virtuous and upright have lived among them and they had not known them for the sons and daughters of the devil that they were?

When Tituba was arrested, she admitted her guilt, and claimed to have ridden on a broomstick high in the sky, and to have her name written in the devil's black book, which she was forced to sign by Sarah Good and Sarah Osborne. According to Tituba, there were nine names written in the book: her own, Sarah Good's, Sarah Osborne's, and six others that she could not read.

It was this revelation that caused pandemonium to break out.

There were more witches than just the three accused by the girls! Who were they? How powerful were they? Did they secretly curse their neighbors and cast spells on their livestock?

There were more arrests made, more accusations hurtled at neighbors in an attempt to save the village from one another.

In the month of March when the villagers' thoughts were normally turned to spring and the planting of crops and the advent of warmer weather, a flood of arrests were made. Martha Corey had scorned the accusations the girls had made and the allegations that there were witches in Salem Village.

"Tis nothing but little girls playing games," she sniffed. "Some people just want attention, if you were to ask me. And as they are getting plenty of it, they are not going to stop with their accusations until somebody stops it for them."

Martha was arrested along with Rebecca Nurse, Rachel Clinton, who lived in Ipswich, and four year old Dorothy Good, the daughter of Sarah Good.

Both Rebecca Nurse and Martha Corey were upstanding and devout members of the community who regularly attended meeting. The accusations against them unleashed a shock wave through Salem Village and Salem Town, where Rebecca (who at age seventy-one was one of the oldest to be accused) in particular was highly respected.

"How can these women be witches?" it was wondered. "They are known to be God-fearing, upright, and respectable citizens."

The general consensus was that if they could be accused of witchcraft, then anyone could be. Thirty-nine prominent members of the community petitioned on Rebecca's behalf, protesting her innocence and her evidences of piety and excellent character. Even a neighbor who had once quarreled with Rebecca, Sarah Holton, defended her and protested her arrest.

The rash of arrests did not alleviate the behavior of the girls. Indeed, it only increased in intensity and it turned out that there were more that joined them, more that joined in those accusations. It appeared that they also had been afflicted. The hunt was on for every witch that they could find.

"Make the witch's cake; make the witch's cake!"

It was an old custom. They took oatmeal and urine from the bodies of the girls who were suffering, and made the cake and fed it to a dog. When it had eaten the witch itself would be afflicted, it was believed, because some of the spell she had cast on the girls would be in their urine and she would then be unmasked and exposed as she suffered the same symptoms she had inflicted on them. And thus was another victim brought to trial; thus was another one sacrificed on the altar of mass hysteria.

Chapter 12
The Quest

The quest was on. Cotton Mather would know no satisfaction until every last witch had been found, every last perpetrator of evil brought to justice, brought to trial, convicted and punished for their crimes. In this quest he presumed that most of the accused were guilty until proven innocent, and spurred the citizens of Salem on in their attempt to purify their community of evil and the forces of wickedness.

He was known throughout New England as a zealot. He wrote more than four hundred pamphlets and books urging the Puritans of the New England Colonies to return to the roots of their forefathers, it being his personal belief that contact with the New World had diluted the strain somewhat.

His father, Increase Mather, was a famous preacher and respected man of God who had also been President of Harvard University, a prize which was denied to his ambitious son; and Cotton moved under his shadow uneasily, always longing to come out from underneath it, always longing to be his own man, always longing to have his name made. And in the crime against humanity that was about to be perpetrated he made his name, and took his place in the halls of infamy.

Cotton would not be satisfied with anything less than the eradication of all evil from the Village and Town of Salem and throughout all of New England. Indeed, he was quoted as saying at the height of the trials, "If in the midst of the many Dissatisfaction among us, the publication of these Trials may promote such a pious Thankfulness unto God, for Justice being so far executed among us, I shall Re-joyce that God is Glorified."

Wasn't this a country that was intended to be full of God-fearing citizens, those who lifted up their voices on the Sabbath and praised the Father above; those that lived their lives to please Him, those who came here from other lands to escape persecution and worship as they wanted to without the government or the Pope dictating the form of service? Did they not long above all else to glorify God?

How then could this have happened? How could this evil have walked among them unaware? Had they been slack in their duty? Had they been faithless in their watch, and failed as watchmen; not being diligent in looking out to guard their hearts and their minds, and very homes and villages from evil?

For it walked among them. It screamed among them. There were accusations flung out. Before this would be over, there would be more than one hundred and twenty men and women, and even children that would be accused of witchcraft. Even little Dorothy Good, just four years old, was accused of witchcraft. Dorothy, it was claimed, had a pet snake that was permitted to bite her, although she suffered no harm from its bite. It was her familiar, said some, just as her mother was accused of consorting with familiar spirits in the forms of birds, as claimed by the slave woman Tituba, so too did little Dorothy consort with this snake in much the same manner.

Soon they began running out of places to put the accused. They began to put them beyond the confines of the jail into isolated buildings under lock and key. The trials were conducted primarily in the Meeting House, an odd location to be tried for one's life in Letitia's opinion. She never thought that the place where the Village worshiped on Sunday in Christian love would be where they hurled accusations against one another on other days of the week. Every accuser was given their day in court. It was not long before people were accusing their neighbors, their enemies, those who irritated them, those they found fault with, of every possible act of evil.

One was accused of inflicting a spell on the Reverend Parris himself.

Remember when the bell was stolen? it was reminded. That was not done by the hand of man, indeed a witch, a servant of Satan, had removed the bell to prevent the good townspeople from coming to meeting on Sunday morning.

Aye, it was agreed, that was an act of witchcraft; that was one putting a spell on somebody to perpetrate that deed and bring about the theft of the bell.

There was another who was accused of inflicting the girls. It was said that Tituba had made little dolls, images of the girls, and she inflicted them with pins. That was what brought about the pain in their arms and their legs.

Every place that she inserted a pin they felt a pain. And indeed, they found such dolls in her room; no one knew why she would possess such a thing except for the practice of witchcraft and evil purposes.

Tituba was the one among them that was different. She had come from the West Indies, and practiced another religion. Indeed, she did not come to meeting with everyone else. She kept to herself as befitted the station of a slave, it had been commonly believed. But now they asked; did she keep to herself because she secretly afflicted the townsfolk with spells and witchcraft?

They began to wonder...

Cotton Mather, after seeing all the floods of accusations and the trials and executions start, began to feel a little qualm, began to feel a little fear. What if they were wrong? What if, despite the evidence of witchcraft that supposedly surfaced at the trials, there were those who were truly innocent?

What if people were merely accusing those whom they disliked, those whom they felt threatened by, those with whom they were at odds? What should they do? How could they test them for solid evidence of their innocence or guilt, in order that they might avoid the wrath of God if they were wrong?

It was at this point that the water test was introduced. An innocent person would sink but a witch would float; for it was believed that water was pure, and would reject one full of evil such as a witch, who was an agent of the devil.

Therefore it was decreed that everyone who was brought to trial would face the water test. Unfortunately, it was too late for those who sank and drowned, but at least their name was cleared.

Well, at least we know they were blameless, said some of those who sought to comfort each other, never daring to admit even to themselves that they were at fault, and that they had accused their neighbor wrongly and had their blood on their hands.

For after all, they were good, honest, and upright citizens who could do no wrong in the eyes of their God.

Chapter 13
Neighbors and Enemies

Letitia increasingly grew afraid as she witnessed the madness that seemed to consume the Village and surrounding towns. She saw far too many people who turned too easily on one another. Indeed, it seemed as though there was a mass hysteria that had broken out and robbed the townspeople of their sanity, of their calm, of their ability to reason. She did not recognize this hysterical, wild-eyed, shrill-voiced group of people in the sedate, prim, and prosaic neighbors that she had grown up among.

What had happened to them? Why had this fear and hysteria overtaken them? Where was the trust in God that they claimed that they had? Why did they feel that they must root out every person that they even remotely suspected of witchcraft?

Yes, it was true that a witch shall not live, according to the Bible. That was what the Word of God said. As witches perpetrated evil and brought harm upon mankind, and consorted with the forces of darkness, they were regarded as those who had rejected God just as the angelic host did who joined in their unholy league with the devil when he tried to usurp the throne of the Holy One. Just as the devil had made war on God and tried to destroy man's destiny, so too a witch brought curses and destruction on those that God loved and wished to bless.

Letitia had no doubt that witches were

real; but did not one have to be confirmed and proved to be a witch in order to be found guilty? Why was it that so many were accused and tried on such flimsy evidence and wild accusations, with no ground in fact to substantiate the truth of the accusations?

How many of these people were actually guilty, she wondered. Were *any* of them?

She shuddered to think of the blood on the hands of her neighbors as they accused and executed randomly those whom they feared or disliked, those that they pointed the finger at and hurled false accusations against. And she shivered inwardly, trying to distance herself from them, hoping to escape the finger herself as she saw the variety of people accused, outrageous accusations;

It was then that Letitia herself started to look at her neighbors with new eyes. What if they were guilty? What if some of them really *were* agents of the devil? What if some of them really did have magic powers, and were able to afflict evil upon their enemies, upon their neighbors, even upon those whom they called their friends?

She found herself regarding everyone around her with suspicion, and found that same suspicion looking out of their eyes back at her. And then fear grabbed hold of her heart, and she thought it would fail her under the terror that she felt. And she felt alone, as she had never felt alone in her life.

What could one do in such a community where everyone was suspect and none regarded as innocent until proven so, and everyone regarded as guilty until the charges against them proved baseless? What could she do to defend herself against such insanity, such a violent outbreak of accusations?

She even began to look askance at her own father and mother.

Why was her mother so insistent that she marry Nathaniel? Did she really desire to make her daughter unhappy? Or did Nathaniel have some kind of hold on her mother? And why did she suddenly find herself warming to Nathaniel although she knew she was in love with Charles?

Was Nathaniel possessed of magic powers? Was he able to make her heart turned toward him through the aid of witchcraft, such as a magic potion? What about that box he had given her; where had he purchased it from? Did it have a spell on it? What about the words to the song he had sung to her? Where had that come from? Was she falling for Nathaniel because of witchcraft that he exercised over her?

She shuddered and inwardly she resolved to force herself to resist his charm, resist his advances, and finally put an end to his courtship. But how to find the courage to do that she did not know, because in truth she wavered and cowered before her mother and father; her father who said little, but looked at her from under thick eyebrows in which unspoken threats of punishment for disobedience concealed hidden danger. She remembered how coldly he had forbidden her mother to help Sarah Good, when all the woman was guilty of was hard luck. Did he regret his cruelty now that the woman was sentenced to death, and just awaiting the birth of a child that would never know its mother before being led away to her execution?

And what of her mother; was she a witch?

All of these accusations and thoughts raced through her mind with the speed and urgency of a herd on a stampede, making her afraid to trust anyone around her. All around her she saw her neighbors attacking other neighbors with accusations, the elderly such as Rebecca Nurse, the outcasts like Sarah Good, and her daughter, like a pack of wolves circling in for the kill, preying on the elderly, the diseased, the young ones who could not defend themselves.

Only to Constance could she speak. Of her fears Only Constance understood. They whispered together one warm July day when washing clothes of the trials and the madness that seemed to have afflicted their neighbors.

"What do you think, Constance?" Letitia asked the other girl. "How can this have happened here in our little community?"

Constance sighed and shook her head as she scrubbed a white towel against a rock.

"I do not know what to think," she replied. "Truly, I am frightened, Letitia. I see everyone around me, people whom I have known all my life, and all calm and reason appear to have deserted them. Anything can happen in an atmosphere like this. Can you believe that so many people have been executed, and that twenty-five more have already been scheduled to come to trial?"

It was, sadly, too true. April had seen a rash of arrests and the accused brought to trial, including the Reverend George Burroughs, the former minister of Salem Village. His arrest shocked Letitia so thoroughly that she was convinced her neighbors had all gone mad.

On June second the official Court of Oyer and Terminer had convened and the first batch of the arrested brought to formal trial. The first to die had been Bridget Bishop, who was hanged only five days after her arrest. Multiple charges of witchcraft was brought against her by several people, who claimed that she used magic to inflict harm on others, and brought much evil to bear against those whom she did not like. She was also accused of an immoral lifestyle, which confirmed the accusation in the eyes of those who tried her case, for did not the corruption of her character bear witness to her guilt?

Sarah Osborne had died in jail before she was brought to trial, proving at least that her claim of ill health that prevented her from coming to meeting was genuine. As she had a history of conflict stemming from legal issues with the Putnam family, some wondered whether the accusing finger pointed at her by young Ann Putnam was directed by the hands of her elders.

As Letitia pondered on recent events she shivered, but not from the cold, although it was a stifling summer day. There was a hint of humidity in the air. The temperatures were stifling, and the days long, and the breeze was mild, but inwardly it was winter. In the hearts of the villagers it was winter as an icy cold seemed to grip their hearts, as they forsook all affection and warmth and liking for each other, and instead focused on survival.

She felt as if she were in a besieged city with none to defend her, climbing higher and higher into a tall tower for self-preservation. And she feared the day when she had no further place to climb.

Chapter 14
Trials and Terrors

At last the day came. Letitia steeled herself to go to the courtroom. It would be considered odd not to attend. She had been excused at the earlier trials due to chores that made demands on her time, but now she had to go, she had to witness this hysteria, the wild accusations. She was appalled at what she witnessed.

Brought to trial at this time were Sarah Good, Elizabeth Howe, Susannah Martin, Sarah Wildes, and Rebecca Nurse.

When they came to trial they stood in the dock and swore before God and man that they were innocent of all guilt, and innocent of any attempt to harm or perpetrate evil upon their neighbors, upon their loved ones, even their enemies. But as each person stood the spectators found themselves watching the behavior of the young girls that had accused so many.

And they determined that when someone was guilty the girls swayed from side to side and cried out as if being afflicted with pain. When that happened the citizens knew that person was guilty as charged and must be taken for the water test. If the girls were calm and reasonable, then that person was clearly innocent and the test was not needed. There were several people who were dismissed in such fashion because the girls had nothing against them. But for those who found themselves in peril of their lives, in danger of losing them, their terror had just begun.

But even the judges saw the ludicrous insanity of the accusation against four year old Dorothy Good and allowed the charge against her to drop. It was widely believed, however, that the little girl had only confessed to witchcraft in order to be with her mother, Sarah Good, the beggar woman who was accused of witchcraft. Too many of her neighbors had witnessed her bad temper, evidenced when they turned her away from their door and heard her muttering curses against them under her breath, for any of them to defend her now. Indeed, they were only too eager to believe that such a one as she was guilty of perpetrating evil and made her a ready scapegoat for the affliction that beset the young girls.

"I was not cursing anyone under my breath," Sarah insisted. "I uttered the Ten Commandments when they turned me away from their doors."

The Reverend Noyes looked at her scornfully and demanded that she recite them before the Court. Sarah turned pale and cast fearful eyes about the room at those gathered against her. She could not recite a single one of the Commandments.

Her doom was further sealed by the accusations arraigned against her.

According to Tituba, Sarah had cast spells on the afflicted girls and forced Tituba to sign the devil's book, and consorted with familiar spirits in animal form that attacked the girls and made them cry out in agony.

Sarah was outraged and denied all the

charges brought against her, insisting that Tituba was the real witch. She did not cower or flinch before her accusers, but rose up in scorn and demanded justice for herself.

When the Reverend Noyes attempted to force her to confess she resisted, repeating her innocence.

"I have done nothing wrong," she stated. "Nor will I stand here and be wrongfully accused!"

It did not take long for the verdict to be decided.

"She is guilty," it was declared by the twelve jurors who convened at her trial, which was short and savage as the "evidence" that in reality consisted of little more than vituperation mounted against her.

Sarah screamed at the Reverend Noyes when the guilty verdict was returned against her, "I am no more a witch than you are a wizard, and if you take away my life God will give you blood to drink!"

"She cursed the Reverend; she is guilty!" cried out the girls, where they sat in the courtroom, witnessing the proceedings.

Sarah was led away to her place of imprisonment, but being pregnant at the time, she would not be hanged until after the birth of her child.

None of those who witnessed her pronouncement on him had any way of knowing that Reverend Noyes would die twenty-five years later of a hemorrhage, and literally swallowed his own blood.

Rebecca Nurse put up a valiant fight for her life and proclaimed her innocence of all charges against her.

Rebecca Nurse was initially judged not guilty, but the citizens of Salem and the accusing girls were outraged at her acquittal and demanded that she be retried. Her second trial returned a Guilty verdict. Such was Rebecca's sterling character, however, that the Governor of Massachusetts, Sir William Phipps, granted her a reprieve. It was a tragic day when the Governor was influenced to rescind it, and Rebecca was led away to the gallows.

Even there she inspired admiration for the calm way in which she met her fate. Her body was cut down and buried in a shallow grave with no marker. She was not permitted a Christian burial, for it was declared, how could one such as she be considered a Christian? Had she not consorted with the devil himself? Her grief-stricken family, however, dug up her body and reburied it in secret, and mourned the loss of a good woman.

Letitia felt as if she were drowning, of swirling in a sea of scandal, hysteria, and terror. It seemed as if the ground underneath her feet had given way, or that she found herself pulled into a current heading out to sea, and she was trying desperately to keep her head above water, to swim for her life. She did not know anyone that she could trust; she did not know if any of the people accused were guilty, or who might be accused next. Indeed, she might be the next one, very likely she would be.

But as the days grew warmer and longer she was able to meet with Charles more frequently and he comforted her greatly.

"Letitia, I truly believe that good will prevail in the end," he attempted to assure her, although she thought she detected a tiny doubt lurking in the depths of his eyes.

"Charles, how can you believe that? Look how many have been accused who are clearly innocent! Look how many have already been executed! Giles Corey, the old man who had all of the stones piled on him and was crushed because he wouldn't confess, and all those who confessed under duress; they were clearly tortured. Who wouldn't confess under torture? Would you be able to resist confessing?"

Charles looked at her soberly without a trace of his customary mischief twinkling in his eyes. Letitia had rarely seen anyone look as grave as her lover did at this moment.

"I do not know," he said solemnly, "and I hope by the grace of God that I never will."

"Charles, this is truly insane; it is madness. What has overtaken these people? It's as if they are terrified for their lives and they are flinging out accusations at anyone in an attempt to save themselves. I've never seen anything like it."

"Nor have I," Charles agreed, "and I have seen many parts of the world. I have seen the West Indies where it is said that occult rituals are practiced, and worship of many kinds elsewhere. But I have never seen this kind of mass hysteria, with accusations of the supernatural against so many.

"The girls who said they saw the specter of one of the accused? And then they took it back and said that it wasn't her, it was someone else. If they were wrong the first time, why do we believe them at all? Why are we listening to them and taking them seriously?"

Letitia shrugged, and then she gave a wry laugh as she was visited by an inspiration.

"Because one of them is the daughter of a minister and she cannot possibly lie because she is a minister's daughter. Nor can her cousin, who is the niece of a minister. They have been brought up as good little girls, and no one is going to dare to say that they are liars."

"Ah!" Charles said softly, "you probably are right. But I shudder for their souls, because if they have accused the innocent wrongly they are guilty of murder; and may God have mercy on them for causing the deaths of so many."

"Aye," Letitia agreed. "I fear for them as well. But I fear even more for those whom they will be flinging their accusations against next and pointing their fingers at. Because those they accuse do not stand a chance, Charles.

"No one is going to say that the daughter of Reverend Parris is a liar, or her cousin, or her friends, because they can do no wrong in the eyes of the villagers. No one would dare to breathe an accusation against them or find fault with them. No one would dare to question their word. To do so would be to invite being an outcast, a pariah, someone who dared to insinuate that the minister and his wife brought up his children wrongly, because that is what it comes down to in the end."

Charles did not reply to her statement. He merely nodded his head and put his arms around her, where she at last felt a measure of calm return to her distressed and anxious soul.

Nathaniel continued to call.

Letitia became increasingly wary as she saw a new determination in his eyes, a resolve to have the question between them settled. And she knew it was only a matter of time before he proposed and she still did not know what to answer. She knew what answer was expected of her, and what answer he expected. He began to assume more proprietorial airs toward her, taking his place beside her after the meeting as if it were his undisputed right to do so. Indeed, he was the only person who would publicly speak to her besides Constance, and for that she was grateful, glad that he was her champion.

But she could not consent to be his wife, not when she felt as she did about Charles. And yet she still could not bring herself to tell her mother about her secret love.

Chapter 15
Pleas and Perils

Something was about to happen. Letitia knew it. She sensed a change in the behavior of those about her. Increasingly, there were those who shunned her, those who refused to meet her eye. Even Constance avoided her at the stream and did not look at her during meeting, did not speak to her in public, and made fewer attempts to visit. Indeed, she seemed to join in the general shunning of Letitia that was exercised against her.

Only Nathaniel continued to call and she secretly met Charles at their usual place in the woods. July gave way to August and the heat of summer intensified, with violent thunderstorms erupting and the threat of hurricanes forming in the ocean on the horizon, suddenly bursting on the shore without warning to wreak havoc and destruction.

And then one day what she had dreaded happened at last.

There was a knock at the door one morning. Her mother answered it, and then Letitia heard a sound of protest and an attempt to bar the way from those who wished to enter, and the sound of a scuffle. Then at last Letitia heard the sound of many feet in the room where she had been sweating in the kitchen over a hot fire as she prepared the breakfast meal of the day for the family.

She glanced up and was startled to see the

town councilmen all assembled, all of them looking extremely somber and serious. In the hand of the most important looking of them all was a scroll which he unrolled once he saw that he had Letitia's attention. He cleared his throat with an important air and addressed her in a booming voice that sounded in her ears like the high tide crashing on the shoreline, rushing in with a mighty force, and taking with it out to sea anything that was unsecured and defenseless from its onslaught.

"Miss Letitia Wood, we of the Council of the Village of Salem, have here a warrant for your arrest issued this day. You will come with us at once, quietly and without protest to the prison we have prepared for you. You will speak to no one as you leave, nor will you contact anyone once you are there. From henceforth you are a prisoner of the Village and await the pleasure of the magistrate who will decide your case."

"No! No!" her younger sister Delilah cried out. "This cannot be! Letitia, tell them they are wrong; tell them it is a mistake."

Letitia turned pale and began to shake violently as her knees threatened to give way beneath her. She moved to her sister's side and attempted to put a reassuring arm around her only to have her arm snatched away by one of the councilmen.

"You will not bewitch this child!" he cried out. "You will do no harm to anyone, anymore. We will see to that, and put an end to your wickedness."

"Now wait just one moment," Letitia's

mother protested, "this child is innocent. I *know* she is innocent. What exactly are you accusing her of?"

"We will address that when she comes to trial," the head councilman told her, as he lifted his head with a disdainful air and assumed a lofty mien. "You are not to speak to her; you are not to contact her in any way. She is a danger to the citizens of Salem and will no longer be permitted communication with anyone henceforth."

And they took Letitia and led her away.

Letitia was so stunned that she couldn't resist. Her knees buckled from under her and at one point she was in danger of collapsing. She fell to her feet only to have two of the councilmen lift her and drag her roughly behind them. She was taken to a lone cabin at the very edge of Salem. They took her there because the prison was now full of citizens waiting for their own trials to come. And so she was placed in isolation until room would be made for her. She was thrown inside and the door locked hastily behind her.

She collapsed and laid on the ground as terrified sobs broke from her. She wondered how she was possibly going to defend herself against what she knew had to be false accusations, knowing how many had been accused during this time of hysteria, only to be disregarded and convicted of wrongs they had never committed.

She thought of Sarah Good, whose only offense against the citizens of Salem Village was poverty; a poverty that was self-inflicted only because she had tried to settle her deceased husband's debt in an honorable way and was then left destitute. If Letitia's mother had not been ordered by her father to stop giving her aid, and instead had been allowed to help her, would she ever have come to trial? Had her father's hardness of heart helped to condemn her to her fate?

Would Sarah have found some measure of respectability if even one of the mistresses of Salem had tried to cultivate in her some semblance of good manners and cleanliness? For it was true that Sarah was often filthy; but in Letitia's opinion how could she be expected to stay clean when she was homeless and did not have access to soap with which to wash herself and only the cold waters of the stream in the woods in which to bathe? Letitia recalled that Sarah had been raised in a respectable family, but she and her sisters were not permitted to claim the inheritance left them by their father, and she had married one man who had brought her nothing but debt, and another who did not lift a finger to save her when she stood on trial for her life.

Tragically, Sarah's baby Mercy had died shortly before she had been tried and hanged. It was rumored that she was malnourished in the prison which she had shared with her mother while Sarah awaited trial. Letitia found herself mourning for this little one who had never stood a chance of survival.

What of the Reverend George Burroughs? If the townsfolk could convince a jury that this man of God was guilty of witchcraft, what chance did she have to convince them of her innocence? Why, none of the village maidens would even speak to her! And she remembered that one of the damaging accusations against Bridge Bishop was immorality, which had sealed her fate.

Rebecca Nurse had been guilty of nothing that anyone could see, except for, due to her partial deafness, misunderstanding a question that was put to her at her second trial, when she made a reference to "one of the women in my company," by which she meant the women who stood trial with her. But the remark was twisted to mean that she meant the coven to which she belonged and where she cast her spells in company with others like her. Such was the atmosphere of hysteria that now ran rampant in the community that she did not stand a chance of failing to be convicted.

As Letitia thought of these people, she knew that her own case was hopeless. Few had spoken to her for some time, except for Nathaniel and her own family, and she was shunned by all of the other maidens in the village, who treated her as an outcast. As such she was on the same footing as Sarah Good; it would not take much for a jury to convict her of whatever lies anyone chose to bring against her at her trial.

She sobbed until she had no more tears in her and then wiped away her tears and quieted herself. She looked around the cabin and took in her surroundings. There was only a solitary window with bars in it to let in daylight; apart from that it was completely dark and no chink of light penetrated the cabin's walls.

As she peered around her gradually her eyes became accustomed to the darkness and she saw at last a table with a candle on it, but she had nothing to light the candle with. There was no fire where she could warm herself, and she was thankful that it was August and therefore not cold.

She knew that she could endure the cold for a while, but she knew she could not endure what she knew was certain to be a trial composed of false accusations against her, with her very existence on the line and her life at the mercy of the citizens of Salem. She trembled as she realized how slim her chances of survival were; indeed, did she stand a chance at all?

Letitia felt overwhelmed with despair as the bleak reality of her situation was borne upon her. She felt that she could not stand anymore of the cold treatment that had already been meted out to her at the hands of the villagers, and was certain that she would experience more of the same at her trial.

And so she collapsed in her isolation as she waited for her trial to come and wondered what would befall her next.

Chapter 16
The Prisoners

After a few days Letitia was allowed out of the isolated cabin and was moved to a larger place where she found herself incarcerated with others who were also accused of the crime of witchcraft and waited for their day in court. The jail was full, so they were confined to a private home that had been turned over to the use of the court during the duration of the trials.

She was relieved to be out of confinement, having grown very lonely and frightened during that time of isolation, where the silence was so intense that it seemed to bear a heavy weight down upon her. She had searched her soul and wondered what she could possibly have done that would cause anyone to accuse her of such a charge, indeed, why anyone ostracized her the way that they did. What had caused her shunning by first the maidens of Salem, and then the citizens of Salem? What had led to this downfall?

She searched her heart and examined it with all honesty and could not find anything of which she was guilty, except for meeting Charles in secret, but no one knew of that. She was sure of it.

And then she remembered with sudden and chilling clarity the time that she had visited Biddy Merriweather and was certain that she had been followed, hearing the sound of footsteps walking behind her. And then there was the night that she had met Tituba and had heard the sound of footsteps behind her on that occasion as well. Had someone followed her secretly?

Or had Tituba betrayed her when she was accused of witchcraft? Was she forced to name those who had come to her for consultation, those who had sought her out to learn magic or perhaps be granted a spell?

And for the first time Letitia was truly frightened, because of *that* crime, she was indeed guilty. She had sought Tituba out; she had practiced divination, which was strictly forbidden in the Bible and therefore by God.

But the frustrating part was that she had not even been able to see the face of the man that she might marry because the wind had ruffled the water and dissolved the image and it was gone forever. She sometimes wondered in her heart if God Himself had brought that wind as a rebuke for even daring to dabble in the dark arts like that. She had always been a good girl, had always followed the rules of the village, had always obeyed the Word of God, and had always sought to learn more about Him. This was the first time that she had strayed, and she began to wonder whether God had actually led her to this place in order to discipline her, remembering that it said in His Word that those whom He loves He disciplines even as a father disciplining a son.

And she trembled in dread as she pondered on her coming trial, and anxiously awaited what the future held, and what fate the villagers would mete out to her.

Now as she joined others who had been accused also, she took stock of their situation and of her own. She looked around and wondered of what these good people could possibly be guilty. She knew so many of them. She knew their deeds and knew that they were good people.

There was Elizabeth Proctor, expecting a child, who had done nothing more than to be the wife of John Proctor, who had derided his servant Mary Warren's claims of seeing the specter of Giles Corey. As Elizabeth's grandmother had been a Quaker and was something of an outcast among her own people in the city of Lynn, it was all too easy for the villagers to declare that the taint had been passed down through the bloodline to Elizabeth. She was charged with tormenting Mercy Lewis by specter, and although a multitude of upstanding and wealthy citizens had filed a petition on her behalf, both she and her husband were accused of witchcraft.

There was old George Jacobs Sr., who had been charged with witchcraft by his own granddaughter in an attempt to save her own life.

Letitia met Mary Eastey, the sister of Rebecca Nurse, who always had a cheerful smile for everyone, was the first to tend to anyone who was ill, the first to feed a hungry beggar, and even give them a change of clothes to keep them warm. The accusations against her were lewd and outrageous, particularly in regard to her Christian character and pious nature, which was well-known to all.

But in the present atmosphere of hysteria that had overtaken Salem and several towns and villages in the surrounding vicinity, there were few who listened to reason, and even fewer who rose up in defense of the innocent.

How could anyone with any faculties for reasoning possibly accuse these people of witchcraft? It was impossible! Had the entire village and towns of the surrounding countryside taken leave of their senses? Were they truly at the mercy of six girls who were not yet even at the age of puberty; who were still children?

And then Letitia wondered why these children were accusing so many people of such horrendous crimes. A flash of insight made her wonder as she considered these girls. Why, the first two to bring their accusations against their fellow citizens were the very ones who had had the strictest regulations of all the children in the village, they were related to the minister. And Letitia wondered if this was an attempt to control their elders, a revenge for being repressed, restricted, and indeed, tied down. Was it a way of showing their power; a way of instilling fear in the adults? Was it a way of letting them know that they held them at the mercy of their hands?

Or had they opened a door to demonic possession, as was claimed by the Reverend Hale, and so had truly experienced torment at the hands of the devil's minions, and accused the innocent by mistake? Had they been the first victims of delusion, which they then infected the townsfolk with to such an extent that they imagined evil everywhere?

Letitia wondered, and as she did so, she wondered when this would all finally cease. When would this madness stop and these accusations quit? Or was it too late at this point? Had Salem become infected with such a poisonous spirit, such a deadly bane of venom, that it would be satisfied with nothing less than the destruction of all those that its citizens regarded with suspicion, jealousy, and envy?

She sighed as she looked around her at those, who like her, were waiting for trial, and knowing that their fate rested in the hands of their fellow citizens and their wild and random accusations.

Chapter 17
Unmasking

By chance it happened one day that Letitia discovered at last what had happened that led to her being shunned by the other maidens of the village, and eventually the townsfolk, and had ultimately led to her arrest.

One of her fellow prisoners had actually nodded to her, giving her a reluctant smile. Letitia remembered that this was one of those who had shunned her the most ostentatiously, who had actually lifted her skirts away from her as she approached, as if she tried to avoid any contamination from Letitia's presence. It was clear that being accused of witchcraft had chastened this woman somewhat; perhaps she was not so judgmental now that she was one accused and waiting to stand trial for her life.

Letitia seized this opportunity to strike a conversation with her.

"Hello, Mary," she said. "How are you?"

Mary gave her a wan smile. She was pale and thin, appearing worn with anxiety, as well she might, being about to stand trial for her life.

"Well, as best as can be expected under the circumstances, I suppose," she answered.

"Yes; it is unbelievable, isn't it?" Letitia asked her. "It is incredible what has happened to the citizens of Salem, that they can believe all of this madness."

"No doubt," Mary agreed. "It is as if the entire village has lost all ability to reason and think clearly, as if sanity has deserted them.

What can possibly have made them doubt the very people they have lived among and grown up with all of their lives?"

"It is outrageous," Letitia stated. "I still cannot believe that I am accused of witchcraft, when I have never practiced or sought anything of that sort in my life."

"Nor have I," said Mary, as she nodded her head in agreement.

They sat in silence for several minutes as they commiserated together, their common accusation producing a bond between them. Letitia felt that at least here was someone who understood how she felt at the injustice of arrest under false charges. And then she posed the question she had been burning to ask for several months.

"Still, I am bewildered," she said, "because for some time now, several months in fact, I have been shunned by most of the maidens of the village. They are not speaking to me and I don't know why.

"Do you have any idea, Mary?"

Mary looked away from her, averting her eyes as she cleared her throat. Letitia felt her heart pound in her chest so fiercely that she feared she would faint. She sensed that Mary did indeed know why she had been shunned. She wasn't certain that she wanted to hear what was said of her; yet she must know in order to defend herself.

"You *do* know!" Letitia stated. "Tell me why; I must know. I do not know of anything that I could possibly have done to invite such treatment. Why am I being shunned, avoided, and ostracized?"

Mary turned red and looked uncomfortable. She appeared flustered, as if she did not know how to answer Letitia's question.

"Please, tell me; I must know," Letitia implored.

She beseeched the other woman with a pleading look that was pathetic to behold, and won her sympathy.

"Alright," Mary said with reluctance as she sighed deeply. "It's because, it has been rumored, that is..what I mean, well, it is said that you have lost your chastity."

She blushed and shed an apologetic smile on Letitia, who was so stunned at the statement that for a moment she could not breathe. For a moment she felt the room swirl around her. Tears sprang to her eyes, tears she attempted to hide from the other woman in an attempt to preserve her dignity.

"What!" she exclaimed in a tone that betrayed her shock.

Her eyes were now brimming with tears at the outrage, the insult, of such an accusation.

"Why would anyone believe that about me? Why?" she asked.

"Well," Mary began, "when the accusation comes from your best friend, I suppose..."

"My best friend! Did I hear you correctly? Did you say my best friend?" Letitia demanded.

"Oh, didn't you know?" Mary asked. "Yes, it is Constance who said that."

Letitia could not believe she had heard correctly. This could not be! Constance would never say such a thing of her; of that she was certain. And yet she felt the room reeling around her. She felt so dizzy that she was in danger of falling. She gripped the nearest object for support, which was a table that stood in front of them near the fireplace in the parlor.

"I cannot believe this. It is not possible. Why would Constance say such a thing about me?"

Mary gave her a sympathetic glance out of warm brown eyes and continued to enlighten Letitia.

"Well, she said that you had been meeting someone in the woods at night; that young man from England that nobody speaks to, Charles Birch."

Letitia was stunned. This was the answer. This was the person who had been following her; not a stranger, not Tituba, but her best friend, the person she trusted above all others in her life. She had followed her when she was unaware and had spread this calumny about her.

"I cannot believe this," Letitia muttered in a sepulchral voice that sounded hollow and far away to her own ears.

She struggled to regain her composure, knowing that others were around them who might observe her behavior and put a negative construction on it and report it at her trial in a futile attempt to save themselves.

"I am sorry," Mary said softly as she laid a hand on the other girl's arm, "but she has been saying this about you for months, and she has been turning all of the other maidens in the village against you."

144

"But why? Why?" Letitia asked. "She is my friend; I trusted her! And it is not true. Yes, I *have* been meeting Charles in secret, but it is just to talk. My parents do not want me involved with him; they want me to marry Nathaniel Stone. So we have been meeting secretly, but all we do is talk; I swear it!"

"Alright, alright," Mary hastened to calm her. "I believe you. But I am merely telling you that this is what has been said about you, and is the reason that you have been ostracized."

"But why would Constance do this? Why?" Letitia exclaimed, feeling a sharp pain in the pit of her stomach as the knowledge of her friend's betrayal began to penetrate her consciousness.

"Well," Mary began, "I can think of an explanation for that. In fact, I can think of a reason for it immediately."

"What is it?" Letitia asked her, as she racked her brain to remember if she had ever offended Constance in any way, wondering what she had ever done to possibly hurt her friend without her knowledge that would lead to her taking this opportunity to strike revenge against her.

Why would Constance do such a thing? How could she possibly have spread such lies and slander against her?

Mary looked at her steadfastly with calm eyes yet sympathetically as she detected the other girl's pain and stunned bewilderment.

"It is because she is in love with Nathaniel," she stated. "If she could get the other girls to believe that you had lost your chastity, they would spread rumors that would eventually reach his ears and sully you in Nathaniel's eyes. And if she could make you look bad in his eyes, then he would lose all interest in you and hopefully would turn his attentions to her.

"That is what I believe to be the case," Mary declared.

"Oh, I cannot believe that!" Letitia exclaimed. "How could she be so false? She is supposed to be my best friend!"

Mary sighed and patted Letitia's hand.

"Well, I have learned that love can do some strange things to people," she told Letitia. "It can either ennoble you, or it can corrupt you. It can expand your heart or destroy your soul. Jealousy is a fearful thing.

"Wasn't it jealousy that led to the downfall of Lucifer? He was jealous of God and tried to take his throne. And then he fell. That, in my opinion, is the root of all evil; jealousy and envy. And it has bitten Constance sorely.

"And that is why you have been shunned, and ostracized, and avoided; because of the jealousy of your friend."

Letitia felt a surge of horror at this revelation. To her dismay she realized that the girls with whom she did laundry was the wolf pack, and that Constance was running with it.

Chapter 18
A Cry For Mercy

The day came at last when Letitia was led into the courtroom, along with all of the other citizens that were being held on the charge of witchcraft. The courtroom had had so many trials over the last couple of months that it was beginning to be known as Witch House. And there she stood before her accusers and, indeed, before the entire village of Salem.

She looked around her at the citizens, hoping to gauge her chances of survival by their countenances. But not one met her glance except Nathaniel; even Constance looked away from her. Letitia was heart sore; her heart was hard as she looked at her false friend, and hoped that she was satisfied with everything she had brought about, at everything she had put her through with her false accusations.

Only Nathaniel looked at her, as her own parents looked straight ahead with stony faces, not daring to smile. Only Nathaniel's eyes were warm and soft, even encouraging. He clearly did not believe the charges against her; and for that she was grateful.

And for the first time she began to wonder if she should have just settled for him. He clearly was a good man who loved her and believed in her goodness and innocence, and what more could a woman ask for than that? And his obvious dismissal of the charges against her demonstrated that rare quality in a citizen of Salem; the ability to think for oneself and not simply follow the herd mentality out of the fear of being labeled different.

At last she stood before the judge who presided over the trials on this particular day.

"Mistress Letitia Wood," he said in a voice as rough as gravel that reverberated through her being as if a death knell had sounded in her ears, "you stand before the entire village of Salem accused of the crime of witchcraft. How do you answer this charge against you?"

"Not guilty!" she erupted, the words tumbling from her lips scarcely before he had finished asking the question. "I am not guilty! Please, I beg you, give me mercy, for I am innocent."

"Enough!" he interrupted. "You will hear the charges brought against you."

Letitia stood waiting for her accusers to come forth and state the charges of which they declared she was guilty.

John Reed came and stood in front and pointed his finger at her.

"Mistress Wood, you put a hex on my child. You put the evil eye upon him on the way to meeting the Sunday before last, and then he came down with a fever. What do you have to say about that?"

"That is a lie!" she cried out. "I never even looked at your child. No one has spoken to me in months; why would I even look at your child?"

"Enough!" the Judge interjected. "Mistress Wood, I am warning you; you will be silent and hear the charges against you. If you interrupt again I will send you back to your confinement to languish there until the end of your days, whether they be long, or whether they be short."

Letitia paled. There was something in the implacable face of the man who held her fate in his hands that told her he would be cruel enough to carry out his threat. She breathed a silent prayer to God for mercy and held her tongue.

Another citizen came forward, old Mistress Holden. She was wizened and nearly toothless, her straggly gray hair persisted in escaping from her cap into thin strands that hung limply about her wrinkled face. She smirked at the young girl and sniffed audibly as she proclaimed her charges.

"Mistress Wood," she said, in a voice as thin as a silken strand from a spider's web, "you have been seen consorting in the woods at night with a young man, and indulging in unchaste behavior with him. No good Puritan maiden would do such a thing; but all know that witches are lewd creatures, engaging in deeds of wickedness. What have you to say about your behavior?"

"That is a lie!" Letitia flared, as her indignation at the connotation on her innocent meetings with Charles gave her courage. "That is a lie; and it is outrageous of you to say that about me! It is a defamation of my character to accuse me of such behavior. All we did was talk; that is all we did, and nothing more. I swear it before God and these witnesses!"

"That is not what has been said about you," Mistress Holden began, only to have Letitia fling caution to the wind and interrupt.

"And I know who has been saying such

calumny about me. I finally know who the culprit is," she said, as she looked boldly at Constance across the room with a challenge in her eyes.

Constance turned pale; her eyes widened and she dropped them before Letitia's gaze. She started fidgeting with her hands, and Letitia knew that she had rattled her. She knew that Constance did not have the courage to stand up and meet her gaze after lying about her.

But there was more to come.

"I know that she has consulted with Tituba, secretly, at night, when all good and innocent maidens should be safely in their beds," said another citizen named Mistress Deborah Plank. "She sought her out and engaged in black magic, and all of the dark arts."

"Is that true?" the judge asked Letitia.

Letitia wavered and swayed on her feet, knowing that she was guilty of this charge. But to admit it would bring a death sentence on her for certain. Yet she had to be honest before God and her peers.

"Well," she began, in a voice that quavered and died in her throat.

She inhaled deeply, cleared her throat, and started over.

"It is true that I did seek Tituba out once. I wanted to know who my future husband would be. I needed to make a decision, and I was torn. I wanted to know whom I was going to marry, and so I asked her to show me."

She glanced apologetically at Nathaniel. She could see clearly even across the room the hurt in his eyes when she had admitted that she met Charles in secret. He was plainly shocked and heartbroken at this revelation of faithlessness from the woman he was courting.

"I thought that I had made up my mind and discovered that I could not, and I could not decide between the two of them. But I have done no more than the other girls who have accused me and all of these others in this courtroom. Those girls have consulted Tituba with the very same question; and worse. They have sought her out for the very same reason and purpose, and have gone even farther to hear about witchcraft and enchantments..."

"That is enough!"

An outbreak of outrage and pandemonium broke across the courtroom. Those present knew that the girls were guilty of such behavior; and the girls themselves were kicking their feet and screaming and crying out.

"She's a witch! She's a witch! She's a witch!"

"We have heard enough," the judge said. "Mistress Letitia Wood, you will be taken back to the isolated cabin where you were first incarcerated, so that you will not contaminate any further your fellow prisoners, or teach them any hexes or spells that they might cast on the good citizens of Salem. You will wait there until the day of your water trial, where you will be further prosecuted. This court is adjourned until I convene it next."

Chapter 19
Nowhere To Turn

Letitia was taken back to the lone cabin where she had first been brought when she was arrested.

Now she knew ultimate despair. She knew she would be judged guilty. She could swim; it was one of the things that designated her as different from the other maidens of Salem. And she had no intention of pretending that she could not and allow herself to sink and in this way be cleared of the charge against her. No, she would swim and fight for her life; but she would still be judged guilty and be hanged as a witch.

She suddenly thought of a stretch of windswept beach where she had spied a lone rose on a cold and windy day of November. It was still vibrantly pink and raised its lovely petals in lone majesty; its glowing green leaves a challenge to the dreary dun sand and the steely gray ocean. Yet it would lose its stand; the cold would eventually shrivel its beauty and snuff out its life, and the waves would make their assault and sweep away its leaves and stem, so that soon there would be nothing left to show that it had ever existed until the return of summer brought forth new blooms once more.

So would it be with her. The fierce tide of the flood of accusations against her would snuff out her life; but unlike the rose, she would not be remembered in Salem Village; no memory of her existence would be permitted to remain. She would not be allowed Christian burial or even a headstone to show that she had ever lived. Such had been the treatment of the others who had been found guilty and hanged; all traces of their existence had been wiped out, and she knew that her fate would be the same as theirs.

Truly she had no way out. There was nowhere to turn.

She sat and pondered on the situation, wondering how she could escape the charges and preserve her life. But no solution was to be found. She would be as those other citizens who were as innocent as she, some even more so, for who among them had sought Tituba out to seek secret knowledge?

The answer was: none of them. Yet they had hanged anyway.

Then she remembered the waves of the sea and how they pounded the coast, sometimes with a gentle rhythm that calmed one's soul, sometimes with a ferocious power that was tantamount to an assault when the wind whipped up the current and sent the waves crashing along the beach during a nor'easter. Yet they were controlled by the limits that were set on them in their onslaught of the shore. Boundaries were established, and their tides were regulated, with only the occasional storm permitted. So it was with how far the enemy was allowed to attack in order to test those whom God loved. In this way were boundaries established and maintained.

Finally, she called on God.

"God, please help me!" she implored. "I am innocent; you know that. You know that I am innocent. Raise up a defender for me; contend with those who contend with me; fight against those who fight against me. Prove my innocence and silence my accusers. Please God; You are all I have. I have nowhere else to turn. Only You can save me."

And she sat on the floor and dropped her head upon her knees and waited for the morning to come.

She was startled out of a fitful sleep by a sound at the side of the cabin. She listened and heard again the sound that had wakened her. There was a knock.

"Pssst! Pssst!" she heard.

What was that?

She rose to her feet and tiptoed over to the side, fearful that a trap was somehow laid for her and was wary of falling into it. But her curiosity was greater than her fear, so she answered the unseen whisperer.

"Who is it?" she whispered.

"It is me, Constance," she heard.

"Constance!" she exclaimed.

Outrage suddenly overwhelmed her as all of the pent up frustration at the ostracism she had endured over the last few months, and her present danger of losing her life found its vent in railing at her faithless friend.

"How *dare* you come here! Go away; I never want to speak to you again! I never want to hear the sound of your voice; your voice that uttered all these lies and false accusations against me that turned the town against me and brought me to this place."

"Please!" Constance cried, "I am sorry. I never thought it would lead to this! All I wanted was for you to have some stain on you so that Nathaniel would leave you alone and end his courtship. He is so upstanding and righteous, a truly godly man. And I thought that if the truth came out that you were meeting Charles in secret that he would be disgusted and turn away from you.

"But I never dreamed it would come to this! Not to standing trial for your life; accused as a witch!"

Letitia was so angry that she clenched her fists together at her side and trembled violently. She dared not speak for fear of what she might say as the hot words of fury threatened to come to the surface like boiling lava from a volcano, erupting and spewing out destruction, leaving devastation on the surrounding landscape. So too could her words destroy her friend, as she was tempted to say wounding things from which Constance might never recover.

She could not believe that her friend could falsely accuse her, and then come to her and say that she never intended it to be as it turned out. Did Constance not realize that once a woman lost her reputation that she lost everything worth having? She lost all chances of any decent man marrying her; and if she did not marry what kind of life would she have? She would be isolated and shunned like old Biddy Merriweather.

"Please," Constance begged, "listen to me. I truly am sorry. And I am asking you to forgive me.

"I am so sorry; I was in love with Nathaniel. I have been in love with him since I was twelve years old. When he chose you I felt jealousy for the first time in my life. And I have repented of it. I have asked God to forgive me; and now I ask you to forgive me as well.

"I have gone to Nathaniel and I have made it right. I told him that you did nothing wrong with Charles. I followed you every time that you went out to meet him and witnessed all of your meetings. I could see the back door of your house clearly from mine. I waited and watched and I followed you every time. I told Nathaniel this, and assured him that you did nothing wrong with Charles: all you did was talk. He understands that, and he has forgiven you."

"Forgiven me?" Letitia queried. "I have done nothing wrong; there is nothing for him to forgive."

"You encouraged the attentions of another man while allowing Nathaniel to court you; you met with Charles in secret," Constance said.

"Yes, that is true," Letitia admitted, "but that is only because my mother would not allow him to court me and kept forcing Nathaniel on me."

"Well, what are you going to do?" Constance asked her.

"Do? What can I *do*? I am in here standing trial for my life. What do you *think* I can do? I really don't have any options, Constance, thanks to you."

"I am sorry, Letitia. I am so sorry," Constance moaned. "Please say that I'm still your best friend! I do truly love you; it's just that

I loved Nathaniel more, and it blinded me. It distorted my soul. I saw you meet Charles and I justified my actions by pretending to myself that only a whore would deceive a man who was courting her by meeting another in secret. But I was wrong.

"Please forgive me; please tell me it will be alright between us."

Letitia sighed. She remembered what Mary had told her about the power of love to ennoble or corrupt one's soul. Clearly it had done the latter to Constance and Letitia was the victim of it. But Constance also saw this and admitted her wrong.

Could she ever forgive Constance for the wrong she had done to her trusting and faithful friend? Did she have an obligation as a Christian to forgive her, even though her behavior was abominable and her attack on her character unjustified? Would God be displeased if she refused to forgive Constance?

Letitia knew full well the answer to that question. Jesus had told Peter that he must forgive his brother not seven times, but seventy times seven. And that one could not approach the altar to worship God unless he first made things right with his brother if all was not well between them.

Still, it was too much to cope with in her present situation. Letitia simply could not deal with these questions at such a time.

"I don't know, Constance," she said, suddenly too weary to hear any more of her friend's explanations and excuses. "I will have to think about it, and at the moment I can think of nothing except how to survive the accusations that your lies have brought against me."

Chapter 20
The Outcome

At last the cries of Constance ceased and Letitia heard a movement outside indicating that Constance had walked away. She had left and gone away.

Letitia sat there contemplating her future and lost all track of time. There was no question of going back to sleep; she was too wide awake now after the visit of Constance. She sat there meditating on her life and events in Salem Village, asking herself if there was anything she needed to ask God forgiveness for before being executed; for she knew this would be her fate.

Finally, though, about two hours after Constance had left her, she heard another sound at the side of the cabin. This was not a soft whisper, but a hammering that threatened to shake the building. And a man's voice came to her ears.

"Letitia," it whispered, "Letitia."

It was Charles!

Her heart leaped in her throat and elation seized her soul. Charles had come; Charles had come to rescue her.

She scurried over to the side of the building where she had heard his voice.

"Yes, Charles; what is it?" she whispered.

"Letitia, I've come to rescue you," he whispered. "You are going to have to climb out of that window."

Letitia was astounded at this statement.

"The window is barred," she informed him,

stating the obvious.

"I am going to remove those bars," he said.

"How?" she asked.

"I have brought someone with me to help," he stated.

"Yes, Letitia; I am here to help," she heard another voice chime in.

It was Nathaniel.

Nathaniel! How could this be? And yet, it was.

"Oh, Nathaniel!" she cried out. "Is that you?"

"Yes, Letitia," he answered. "I have come to help Charles rescue you. Be calm; we are going to get you out of here."

"Oh, Nathaniel," she cried as tears sprang into her eyes, "you are so good and so kind. What must I do?"

"We are going to get you out. Nathaniel has some tools that we can use to dismantle the metal grille and remove it to open the window. Once we have accomplished that we will pull you out from this window and get you away to safety. Just stand back while we go to work and take care of this."

She heard some scuffling and a slight tapping sound of metal against metal. She prayed silently that no one would hear the sound and come to investigate, and arrest those who attempted to come to her aid. The sound continued, and after a while she heard something break. She looked up and saw that the metal grille that held the bars in the window had broken away and the window was completely clear.

And then she saw two arms reaching in the window for her. It was Charles. She ran over to the window. She allowed him to take her by the arms. Charles pulled and pulled, and behind him, Nathaniel held onto his waist and anchored him securely to the ground. Between the two of them they lifted her out of the window and out of her prison.

"Oh," she exclaimed as she collapsed into Charles' arms.

Charles held her close and bent his head over hers protectively and clutched her tightly as if he would never let her go. He kissed her brow fervently. Nathaniel flinched as he watched; then averted his eyes as their caresses grew more intimate, Charles kissing her cheeks, and Letitia stroking his hair. And then she caught herself up and remembered her other rescuer.

"Oh, Nathaniel," she said, "thank you so much for helping Charles get me out of here."

"I would do anything for you, Mistress Wood," Nathaniel said with a sigh. "When Constance came and explained what happened, I immediately forgave you."

"And I knew about these bars and how they could be removed," Charles stated, "but I lacked the tools to do it by myself. So I went to Nathaniel, whom I knew as a blacksmith would have what was needed and we buried our differences; and between the two of us we decided to get you away. Your safety matters to both of us more than anything."

Letitia felt tears spring into her eyes once more as she gazed at the two men who stood before her, both of them so valiant, both of them loving her steadfastly.

"Thank you both for rescuing me," she stated. "You have saved my life."

She suddenly felt chilled as she realized how close she had come to death, and her knees buckled. Charles caught her hand and pulled her up, putting an arm around her to steady her. She smiled up at him gratefully and then turned her attention to the problem at hand.

"But what can I do? I cannot go back home; I would only be arrested again, and this time probably put to death before even given the water test."

"No, you cannot go back home. You are right; if you do you will only be arrested again and probably executed immediately, as it will be said that only a true witch could have escaped such a stalwart prison," Charles said. "We have come up with another way. I bought passage for you on a ship that this very night will take you to Boston, and I am going with you. I am putting Salem behind me and I am never coming back."

"That is best," Nathaniel agreed. "Get away and make a fresh start. I will take full responsibility for your escape. I will tell them what has happened, and I will condemn them for daring to accuse you of any wrongdoing. Constance has assured me that she will go also and confess that she lied about you."

"And what will happen to her?" Letitia queried.

She knew that the penalty for false accusation was very strict, and she feared for Constance, even in the midst of her anger toward her.

"Well, if I can arrange it she will have no more than a day in the stocks," Nathaniel answered. "She will be humiliated, but not harmed. And it will serve her right to experience a taste of what she put you through when she deliberately smeared your reputation in the eyes of the village. So too shall she be on public display, and know what it feels like to lose public respect."

Letitia was satisfied.

"Alright, then," she said.

She wondered in her heart whether she would ever be able to forgive Constance for what she had done. Still, Constance *had* gone to Nathaniel and confessed what she had done and made things right with him. And between Nathaniel and Charles, the two of them had brought her out of her prison and into safety.

Letitia stood on the shore in the dawn of a new day. Fingers of rosy sunlight were tentatively creeping up over the horizon, shedding a pearly gleam on the ocean that appeared pale gray in the early morning light. White capped waves lapped gently on the rocky shore and against the stones that rose here and there out of the ocean depths near the coastline.

Letitia breathed in the vista before her, thankful for the sight of what she thought she would never see again. A ship stood before them, the gangplank down and waiting for passengers to board for their voyage. The realization suddenly struck her; she was going away, away from Salem at last! And excitement stirred within her, even as she sorrowfully considered all those that she was leaving behind...

Would she ever see her mother or father again? Would they dare to come to visit her in Boston; or would they fear what might happen to them if it were discovered that they had dared to seek out their disgraced daughter? And what of her sister; would she see her grow into a young woman, know the nieces and nephews that would be born in the years to come? And Constance; was it possible to mend their friendship and return to the old relationship?

But no; of this last Letitia was certain. Trust had been broken, and a side of her friend that she did not know existed had been exposed. Jealousy had overwhelmed Constance to the point that she had willfully sought to destroy her; was it possible to forgive such an act? And yet she knew in her heart that if Jesus were standing here in front of her He would tell her to do just that. She pondered and she wondered...

At last she became aware that it was time to board. She turned to Charles, who stood beside her, smiling at her tenderly. She leaned against him, deeply thankful that she had such a champion. And then she looked at Nathaniel, who had accompanied them to the harbor, as if reluctant to let Letitia out of his sight.

She gazed at him now and saw that his devotion was unchanged; his eyes still shone with warmth and tenderness. And she felt a pang of regret for hurting him, and found herself wondering what her life would have been like had she accepted his wooing and become his wife.

But in the instance of wondering she knew. Her life would have been like that of every woman in Salem; a good and dutiful wife who raised the children, cleaned the house, cooked the meals, and never gave a thought to anything more, never wondered if life held any other purpose or destiny. She would have been earthbound, and never left the village to explore the world outside.

And for the first time she felt assured that she had made the right decision in choosing Charles. Both he and Nathaniel were good men who loved her with an unshakeable devotion. Yet with Nathaniel she would have been tied to the ground; with Charles she could soar.

In her dream about the two trees lay the answer to he dilemma. Both of the trees were good, each in its way. The one shorn of leaves was upright, perfectly formed, with nothing to hide. Such was the righteousness of Nathaniel, a good and devout man.

The other tree was full and lush with leaves that offered protective shelter from danger. But the leaves also invited exploration, and hinted of wonders to be discovered. Here then was the answer to the riddle.

Both of her suitors were good men. Her choice lay in whether she desired safety or adventure. With Nathaniel she would have been a respected citizen of Salem; with Charles she found her true mate, an explorer with whom she could share adventure.

A thought struck her suddenly; Nathaniel had the tools that Charles needed to release her from her prison. Had Nathaniel not been courting her and willing to do anything to save her, Charles would not have had the aid that was needed to break open the metal grille and release her. For the first time she saw the providence of God in Nathaniel's courtship and she marveled at how He truly worked all things together for good for those that love Him, just as he promised in His Word.

When they reached the ship, Nathaniel bowed and raised her hand to his lips. He dared for the first time, in this moment of parting, to kiss it. He gave her one last wistful smile, a trace of tears glimmering in his dark eyes, and then bowed to Charles and left them. The morning mist quickly swallowed him and he was lost from view.

Charles turned to her and smiled, a light leaping into his eyes that seemed to Letitia like the first star of the evening shedding its light on a darkened world.

"Well, Mistress Wood," he said, "are you ready for your journey to Boston?"

Letitia returned his smile and nodded her head vigorously.

"I am," she said. "Ready for Boston and any other journeys we might take; wherever our road may lead us."

Chapter 21
Aftermath

Later from the safety of Boston Letitia heard news about Salem and what had transpired.

Not long after her escape the Reverend George Burroughs had been convicted and sentenced to death. He recited The Lord's Prayer as he was led to his execution. As it was believed that witches could not say The Lord's Prayer a seed of doubt was planted in the minds of Salem's citizens for the first time.

Then the day came when the girls went too far with their accusations. They claimed that the wife of the Governor of Massachusetts, Lady Mary Phips, was a witch. It was at this point that the Governor ordered an end to the proceedings.

There had been more than one hundred and twenty accused, with twenty found guilty; although it was doubtful that any of them were. And of those who stood trial Letitia knew that only Tituba was truly guilty of anything through the practice of divination and the black arts.

And yet Tituba had all charges dropped against her and she was released. She was eventually sold back into slavery and shipped out of the Americas.

And that was as near to true justice as any of the victims of the Salem Witch Trials ever got.

Repercussions continued for years. Cotton

Mather found himself at the center of a firestorm, his rhetoric being held partly to blame for the slaughter of so many innocents, and the destruction of the lives of those who had been accused and released, only to discover that they were considered outcasts because of the taint of accusation upon them. Increase Mather summed up the prevailing opinion of those outside the environs of Salem with his words that "It were better that ten suspected witches should escape than that one innocent person should be condemned."

It was some years later when one of the young girls who had initiated the accusations came forward and confessed that she had been wrong.

Ann Putnam was left an orphan seven years after the trials when her parents died suddenly, leaving her to raise nine siblings. Her life was a hard one, and she did much soul searching regarding her part in the accusations. In the year 1706 she publicly apologized for what she had helped to set in motion.

"I desire to be humbled before God for that sad and humbling providence that befell my father's family in the year about ninety-two; that I, then being in my childhood, should, by such a providence of God, be made an instrument for the accusing of several people for grievous crimes, whereby their lives was taken away from them, whom, now I have just grounds and good reason to believe they were innocent persons; and that it was a great delusion of Satan that deceived me in that sad time, whereby I justly fear I have been instrumental, with others, though ignorantly and unwittingly, to bring upon myself and this land the guilt of innocent blood; though, what was said or done by me against any person, I can truly and uprightly say, before God and man, I did it not out of any anger, malice, or ill will to any person, for I had no such thing against one of them; but what I did was ignorantly, being deluded by Satan.

"And particularly, as I was a chief instrument of accusing Mistress Nurse and her two sisters, I desire to lie in the dust, and to be humble for it, in that I was a cause, with others, of so sad a calamity to them and their families; for which cause I desire to lie in the dust, and earnestly beg forgiveness of God, and from all those unto whom I have given just cause of sorrow and offense, whose relations were taken away or accused."

Those victims who had survived her accusations, and the families of those who had lost their lives as a result of them, extended the grace of God to Ann and forgave her for the harm she had inflicted upon the innocent.

In time Salem came to admit the collective wrong they had done in those mad and fevered days in 1692. In 1703 the Reverend Joseph Green and the members of his congregation voted to reverse the excommunication of Martha Corey. Eight years later the General Court of Salem reversed judgment against many of those who had been convicted.

None of the other girls who had started the accusations repented or apologized to the victims, living or dead, or to their families.

But it was too late for those people. It was too late for those good citizens. It was too late for the innocent.

And thus the infamy of Salem lived on.

A message from L. M. Roth:

If you enjoyed this story, please leave a review on Amazon, Goodreads, or other websites of your choice so that other readers may discover it as well. Thank you.

L. M. Roth is the pen name of a Christian author from the American Midwest. L. M. Roth is a "pilgrim on the path of life" and a seeker of truth. This quest first began at the age of eight when the author read Little Women and was struck by the sense of destiny shared by each of the March sisters as they "pilgrimed" their way through the trials and thrills that only life can offer. The quest deepened through the exposure to classic mythology and legends, which birthed a sense of hidden identity, that we are not who we have always thought we were, but are each of us heroes and heroines destined for something great and noble.

Who are we? Where are we going? What tasks are we meant to accomplish during our time on Earth? We are all on a journey together as we seek the answers. You may join L. M. Roth in that quest anytime you read one of the author's books.

Books by L. M. Roth include:

Quest For the Kingdom Part I The Legend of the Great Pearl

Quest For the Kingdom Part II Conquering the Domain of Darkness

Quest For the Kingdom Part III Invitation To Eternity

Quest For the Kingdom Part IV A Stranger Among Us

Quest For the Kingdom Part V Rise of the Time of Evil

Quest For the Kingdom Part VI The Sorceress and the Seer

Quest For the Kingdom Part VII A New Kingdom Rises

A Dance In the Desert The Story of Leah, Jacob, and Rachel

A Hope In The Dead of Night The Story of Ruth

A Knight's Guide To Spiritual Warfare

A Star In the Darkness Esther and the King of Persia

Abelard and the Dragon's Vapor

Abelard and the Witch's Vengeance

Abelard and the Knights' Vow

Arise My Love The Princess Who Fell Asleep

Battleground: Elijah and the War With Jezebel

Beware My Lady The Princess Who Would Not
Wed

Cinderella's Shoe A Fairy Tale Murder Mystery

Come Back My Lord The Princess Who Loved
Too Much

Disenchanted In the Land of Dreams Come True

Dragon Slayers and Other Tales From the
Perilous Forest

Lights in the Mist and Other Original Fairy Tales
and Fairy Tale Spoofs

Christmas Cheer and Other Holiday Stories

CPSIA information can be obtained
at www.ICGtesting.com
Printed in the USA
FSHW020503181021
85542FS

9 781977 637376